PEMA DONYO
Author of *One Last Letter*

Revolutionary
Hearts

Crimson Romance
New York   London   Toronto   Sydney   New Delhi

CRIMSON
ROMANCE

Crimson Romance
An Imprint of Simon & Schuster, Inc.
1230 Avenue of the Americas
New York, NY 10020

For information about special discounts for bulk purchases, please contact Simon & Schuster Special Sales at 1-866-506-1949 or business@ simonandschuster.com.

The Simon & Schuster Speakers Bureau can bring authors to your live event. For more information or to book an event contact the Simon & Schuster Speakers Bureau at 1-866-248-3049 or visit our website at www. simonspeakers.com.

ISBN: 978-1-4405-9087-0
ISBN: 978-1-4405-9088-7 (ebook)

To my mother and father, for allowing me to grow up on a steady diet of historical romance novels.

Acknowledgments

Huge thanks to Tara Gelsomino for taking a chance and supporting my offbeat idea, and a colossal thanks to Julie Sturgeon for her keen editorial eye. Your endless support and offered help during the entire editing and publishing process is much appreciated. I extend my heartfelt admiration to the Crimson Romance artists as well, who never to fail to create some of the most eye-catching covers!

Thanks to you too, Kelsang, who I know would rather read a dystopian sci-fi thriller than a historical romance novel. When you said you liked this one, that was one of the best compliments ever.

And thank you to all my readers—this one's for you.

Chapter One

1924

What in the blazes was he supposed to do?

Warren read the wrinkled letter again for the thirtieth time that afternoon. The paper had faded yellow from its long journey across the Atlantic and had become creased in too many places to count. The shorthand method was familiar to him, but the contents of the letter were not.

He cursed beneath his breath. His previous years spent in the National Bureau of Criminal Identification investigating domestic anarchists hadn't been this difficult. At least he would be able to dash away on a moment's notice, unseen and unheard. The U.S. government had placed him as a blasted British general! He couldn't just slip away anymore.

Where was the nearest other U.S. operative, anyway? Lucknow, most likely. But that was more than 300 kilometers away. He couldn't steal one of the cars without the other soldiers running after him. And Lucknow was hardly a short motorcycle ride.

Warren pressed the letter against the oak table, his fingers running along the folded creases of the missive. He interpreted the shorthand as he read it aloud to himself, if only to confirm the message was true. Perhaps he had misread. "Agent, we regret to inform you that we have reason to suspect your identity has been compromised. The NBCI has folded into the FBI. Find a way to return home."

He crumpled up the letter and shoved it into the roaring flames stoking in the marble fireplace. *Home.* Back to America. How on earth did they expect him to do that?

Warren rubbed his jaw with his hand, placing one elbow over the mantel. He had no time for this, not when he didn't even have information to report back to the NBCI yet. They'd sent him to ferret out rumors that one of the Indian revolutionaries was an anarchist with the potential to influence rebels back in the States. What was his mission now that the bureau had become absorbed into the Federal Bureau of Investigation? He'd heard whispers of what the organization did, of course, and he assumed it was more than catching anarchists. But without any direct contact with the bureau, only the devil knew what the FBI would want him for. Did he still have a job? The Indians had only started to voice civil unrest, and there was so much knowledge yet to be discovered.

His eyes wandered to the open window. Wispy, white curtains framed the view outside his mansion, where he could see the tops of houses from the nearest village. *There.* That was where he needed to be. That was where all the real action was happening, not shut inside the safety of marble walls.

"*Sahib?*"

He looked up at the sound of his butler's voice. The Indian bowed before him, his turban shaking a bit as he stood back up. The man kept his eyelids hooded, avoiding direct eye contact with his employer.

Warren winced. As much as he'd tried to acclimate himself to the British colonial culture, he never understood the servant system here. It was no better than the old slavery back in the States.

"What is it?"

"The gardener has brought a new maid for you."

He raised a brow. "When did I request a new maid?"

"He says you will not turn her away, *sahib*. She is to replace one of the older maids who works here."

In the passing seconds, the orange flames hissed and crackled in the fireplace as they eroded the logs. The contents of the letter were stored away as nothing more than dust and ash, and his message from home had faded into smoke.

So had his hard-won position undercover.

"Send them in." What did it matter, a new servant or an old servant? Neither was going to help him maintain his position. How could anyone have suspected him? It certainly wasn't the way he portrayed himself. His British accent had become nearly second nature. He barely remembered what he sounded like without it.

His fists clenched, straining his upper arms in the starched general's uniform he wore. How on earth could the NBCI not send him any instruction on how to return home?

The turbaned servant bowed once more. His slippers padded softly against the marble flooring as he exited the room. The floor was nearly as elegant as the rest of the ballroom, complete with a crystal chandelier, gold-leafed accents, and colorful murals that would rival the works found in St. Peter's Basilica. He had to admit that when he'd stolen the real general's identity, he hadn't expected a house quite so opulent. It would be difficult leaving such a lavish place. Maybe the NBCI had it wrong. Maybe his identity wasn't compromised...yet.

"General Carton, *sahib*, this is my sister."

Warren turned his attention away from the comfortable palace he'd learned to call home and toward the gardener. He recognized Raj...the one whom his chain in command had told him to keep an eye on. Raj Singh had risen to fame in the record books of the National Bureau of Criminal Identification as an anarchist determined to overthrow the British government. He'd started to gather quite the following, the bureau had been alarmed to find out. Their brilliant idea had been to dispatch Warren as a British general. He found the idea laughable in retrospect. Yes, of course, the British general would be informed of all the revolutionaries' secrets.

"Raj." He nodded to his gardener and then turned his attention to the woman standing next to him. She was several inches shorter than Raj and slighter in build. A long veil covered her head, and a faded red sari draped over her slim shoulders. "Lower your veil."

The girl dropped her veil. He studied her with the quick precision of an operative scanning a target.

Her Eurasian skin was tan, not quite as dark as the other Indian maids in his house but not light enough to be British. Half-Indian, he guessed. He'd heard during his training that they were rare, but his time in India had proved quite the opposite. She looked like she was in her mid-twenties. Her dark, wavy hair fell to her shoulders. Her thick eyebrows were high and arched, her lips full and plump. Though her veil had been covering her face moments before, she stood with her chin tilted upward. Pride shone in her eyes as she met his gaze with a challenging look.

"Parineeta Singh. She will serve as the new maid in place of our grandmother."

"Hello, Miss Singh," Warren began in Hindi. "Why do you wish to take your grandmother's place here?"

Her eyes flashed with an emotion he was surprised to decipher as anger. Before he could apologize, she responded in British-clipped English, with nearly no trace of an accent. "She has served enough of her time in this prison. It is my turn to take her place." She bit her lip immediately after her response, as if afraid of what she'd say if she continued speaking.

Raj elbowed his sister.

Warren held up his hand. "It is quite all right." A corner of his mouth twisted upward. She was not simply any maid after all. "What makes you so convinced this is a prison, Miss Singh?"

She remained silent.

"Go on," he encouraged. Now this was the information he needed to report back to the National Bureau…FBI, he corrected. Damn, he needed to find out what this new FBI wanted him for. No more battle plans or details of rebellions; he'd had enough of those. He needed real accounts from Indians about the effects of this anarchist's leadership.

"The way you treat us as racially inferior."

"I should hope not. And how do you know such flawless English?"

"My mother taught it to me." Learned it from her British soldier, Warren presumed. The girl looked away from him and toward the marble floor. The challenging expression was still set by the fierce look in her eyes, but she seemed to be trying to displace it somewhere else.

He narrowed his eyes at her. Her hands were clasped behind her back, and her head was turned slightly downward now. There would be no more information from her today. But she was spirited. She was willing to share the details he needed. And she was, he noted, Raj's sister. If he could not gain information from Raj himself, she would be the next best source. *Perhaps I will return home with useful information after all.*

"Miss Singh, I do not think I want you as a household maid." Warren smiled. This would work out very well. "You will assist me, and me alone, in my study."

The girl looked up; her large, brown eyes widened in surprise and her lips parted slightly, but she said nothing.

"My study is in that direction." He pointed down the hall. "That is all. Thank you," he added in Hindi to Raj.

Warren couldn't resist one last peek at the fireplace. Miniature marble columns flanked the collection of ashes and flame on both sides. No traces of the letter. For now, his identity was safe.

His footsteps echoed on his walk to the study. The framed portraits of British generals before him lined the walls. Their images looked the same, one after another: brown uniform, handlebar mustache, judgmental gaze at Warren's disguise.

The Anglo-Indian girl's pretty face as she dismissed him on her way out of the room flashed through his mind. He furrowed his brow. When had he ever cared for women's looks when on a mission? Her appearance didn't matter; her words did.

Judge me now, he wished to say to the paintings. For however long his mission would last, he would not return to the States empty-handed. He hadn't just found a maid—he'd found a source of information.

• • •

"What was it? What did he say?" Raj grabbed Parineeta's shoulders and whirled her around to face him.

"I..." She rubbed the back of her neck. "I am to help him in his study?"

"Perfect!" Raj grabbed both of his sister's hands. His weathered palms squeezed her smooth ones. "I want you to remember everything he says, all right? Anything he says about our independence movement...I want you to remember it all."

A sense of unease gathered in her gut. She knew her brother had always wanted an inside perspective of how the British assessed the growing noncooperation movement. "But he did not ask me to be his maid. I have no training to assist in office work."

Her brother rattled on. "*Aye Bhagwan*, this has worked out better than I'd hoped."

She scratched the back of her ankle with her other foot, shifting her weight. It didn't make any sense. She nibbled her lower lip. "Why would he ask me, though?"

Raj shrugged. He leaned against the doorway of their grandmother's house, one hand resting on the wooden frame.

"Why does it matter? The gods have chosen you to help us win our freedom! Don't you want that?"

She stepped inside the house, passing through the cramped kitchen. "Of course I do, I just..." She could have sworn the sparkling crackles of a flame had singed the air when she spoke to General Carton. She'd half-expected him to strike her for disobedience. The same punishment happened to countless other girls when they spoke out against a British master or made a mistake. Why had he looked amused when she spoke instead?

"This is your purpose in life, Nita. Never forget that. This is how we avenge the death of our mother, the abandonment of your father..."

She bristled at the sudden mention. The deceptive scum of a British soldier who'd abandoned her mother when he found out she was pregnant? She'd heard the story only too many times from their mother before her passing.

"I know, Raj."

Her brother stayed in the doorway, surveying her. Ambition gleamed in his brown eyes. "Remember when you used to follow me to revolutionary meetings?"

She'd been but a child at the time. Her gaze shifted in the direction of the other small houses in the village, covered in dust and still exactly the same as fifteen years ago. "Whatever happened to those meetings?"

"The previous general who lived here suspected us. We meet in a neighboring village now." He lifted his chin. "Would you like to join us at the next meeting? Not as an observer but as an active participant?"

The heady rush of Raj's invitation washed over her. Her bare feet stood still in the swirling dirt as the scorching rays of the sun beat against the back of her neck. "Why?"

"You are a woman now. You will help us win this fight. You will help us defeat this foreign ruler and all the other men like him who seek to deny us independence."

The general's blue-green eyes hadn't conveyed an angry man who would command troops on the palace grounds or one who barked orders to his Indian servants. His eyes seemed...kind. Parineeta shook her head. She couldn't let herself be distracted. Kind or not, this man was capable of dangerous things.

She hadn't found a job; she'd found a way to help free her country.

Chapter Two

"Please sit down, Miss Singh." Warren gestured to the chair on the other side of his desk.

Her movements were hesitant. The large, beautiful eyes scanned the room with expert precision and quick speed, as if she were documenting and memorizing every object in his study.

"Sit down. I insist."

Parineeta finally settled into the wooden chair upon his second request. She lifted up the edges of her sari to set the cloth over the end of the seat. The skin between the end of her *choli* sleeve and her wrist soon disappeared as the drape of the cloth covered it. Her glossy, dark hair was covered once more as she gathered the veil back over her head.

A beat of silence. Warren drummed his fingers against the top of his desk. Interrogations were a part of his training, but usually the suspected anarchists questioned were already under custody. Never did he take a course in how to interrogate a female servant while in disguise.

"Well, Miss Singh, what is your impression of me?" He winced in regret at his choice of words the moment they left his mouth. While the accent sounded convincing, the words did not. Other British generals never seemed as bold as he was.

Her eyes flashed. With surprise or with amusement, he wished he knew. "What do you mean, sir?"

"The British. What do you think of the British?" Warren folded his arms and placed his elbows over the top of the table. There, that was better. Assert his authority, settle back into the disguise and gain her trust. Nearly a year in India and he had yet to hear reliable information about the extent of Raj's anarchist influence.

This fiery girl was his one chance at a glimpse into her brother's activities.

"I believe they all think very highly of themselves."

"And you do not, I assume?" The brass buttons from his regiment uniform pressed against the oak desk as he leaned forward.

The girl's eyelids were hooded as she spoke. "I do not believe any race is better than another or that one race is entitled to freedom while another is not."

"We bring civilization, Miss Singh."

"What civilization—the railroads? The business that takes money from us and sends it back to England?"

"We bring needed modernization to your society."

"Your people act as lords over us, demanding our crops and taxes. Our society was just fine without your people before, and it will exist just fine when your people leave!" Parineeta looked up; the fierce lightning in her eyes could have struck him down cold. Then she glanced away, training her gaze back on the wooden floorboards. The outburst was replaced by a calm temperament. "Sorry, sir. I do not know what came over me."

He suppressed the urge to laugh. She would never have fit in as a housemaid, not with that fire.

"Miss Singh." Warren pulled his fountain pen closer to him. He began scrawling on a nearby piece of paper, writing out her name. "Parineeta, is it?"

The girl nodded.

"Good. I am documenting a…project of sorts." Should he trust her with his mission? Oh, not the spying part, of course, but could he ask her straight out? Moving too quickly on the first day could arouse her suspicions…or it could be the first step toward a treasure trove of information for the bureau—damn, the FBI. Still, it was worth the risk.

"I need your help documenting what the Indians think of British colonization."

"Pardon?"

Warren set down the pen and massaged his temples with his thumb and forefinger. "I need your help, I'm afraid. None of the other servants will talk to me about the conditions of the Indians here. I need to give the report back to my field marshal in the British Army so that they have a better understanding of the effects of long-term colonialism." It was half-true. Replace "British" with "American" and he'd be able to swear the honesty of his words to a priest.

"I do not understand. Why would you want my opinion?" Panic settled in the girl's expression. She tilted up her chin in a brave front, but he could detect the uncertainty.

"Because I am working on a research project." Warren adjusted his high, starched collar, tugging at the end of it to increase the space between his neck and the cloth. He would never get used to the discomfort of British uniforms.

"Why would you need my opinion?"

He clasped his hands together over the paper. "For one, your English is flawless. I doubt any ideas will be lost in translation." And damn it all, her English ability led to his best chance at having enough information to report to the bureau. If he wanted a job with the new FBI, it wouldn't help to have never completed his mission with now-defunct NBCI. "You are my servant and, therefore, my employee. That is how you will serve me in this house. Is that all right?"

The girl's eyes suddenly widened. "No!"

"No? I am trying to work with you, not…" He pushed his chair back when she stood up. Parineeta had one hand clasped over her mouth and the other hand pointed in the direction of his window. He followed the direction of her gaze to a man outside.

He gasped. Several of his soldiers were beating Raj.

"What in the devil…" He swung back around at the sound of a bang. The oak door still swung from where Parineeta had flung it open. Only the back of her sari was visible as she dashed down the hall, her footsteps clattering across the blue tile.

Chapter Three

Parineeta's bare feet slapped against the dirt, causing plumes of fine dust to rise up with each step she took. "*Roko*! Stop, please stop!"

The British soldiers continued to strike Raj, using their fists to cause her brother to stagger backward into another group of waiting soldiers behind him. Red liquid streamed out of his smashed nose. The soldiers' beige uniforms were stained crimson with his blood, covering their brass buttons with a lethal paint.

Her cries remained unheard. She launched herself at one of the soldiers and tried to pry his arms off her brother. In a moment, she found herself flung backward. The heavy blows continued. Kicks and cries became lost in the dangerous dust. "*Roko*!"

The last time her brother had returned home bashed and bruised, it was because he'd been struck by club-wielding police during an event that had begun as a nonviolent protest. One of his friends had died from head injuries. Parineeta had thanked the gods that her brother had remained all right, but he'd since turned away from nonviolent methods. Had he used his fists against these soldiers?

Before she could fling herself into the fray again, a long shadow swept over the ground, covering her own figure and the shapes of some of the soldiers. The man behind her was tall, broad-shouldered, and...

"That's enough!"

Her shoulders drooped at the sound of the voice. Without warning, her heart started hammering against her ribcage. Why was he here?

The soldiers dropped Raj. Her brother fell to the ground with another cry and doubled over in pain. She rushed forward, grabbing his limp form and rocking him against her chest. Blood trickled out of both nostrils. His upper lip had already begun to swell, and she could make out the beginning of a nasty bruise on his cheek. Yet he was still conscious. No sign of a head wound, either. A sigh of relief escaped her lips.

"Who said you could beat this man? This man works for me, just as you do." General Carton barked out the scolding at his soldiers. "Now tell me why you took it upon yourselves to harm him!" His expression grew dark as he shouted his command at the men.

Parineeta had never seen men in uniform look so frightened. Their formerly brazen stances and behavior were replaced by slumped shoulders and downcast looks. He seemed to make them shake inside their polished boots.

One of the men stepped forward. "The…the darkie asked for it, sir. He called us his jailers."

"It does not matter what he calls you." The general scowled. The bright sun rested behind him, framing his outline in a burst of white light as he stood there. "Extra practice for all of you at sunrise. No one harms my workers; is that clear?"

The men nodded. A collective gulp could be heard.

"I said, is that clear?"

"Sir, yes, sir!" the men all chanted in unison. They saluted and then marched away from the general, postures squared and heads hung low.

Parineeta felt her brother's weak body flagging in her arms as his weight sank against her. "Raj!" She tried to shake him, but there was no response. His head lolled back against the top of her forearm.

"Go get him treated."

As she peered up at him, his fists remained clenched at his sides, but his expression seemed calm once again. All traces of the fearsome general had vanished. The man possessed two completely different sides. "Why did you help him?"

He frowned, as if the answer was obvious. "I couldn't stand around and watch a defenseless man nearly die."

"Most British officers would."

Their eyes locked, a steel blue-green gaze fixed onto hers. Against her will, her heart skipped a beat. "I can assure you I'm not like most officers."

"Thank you, sir."

"You have nothing to thank me for." The general started to walk away but then stopped suddenly and looked over his shoulder. The man ran one hand through his black, wavy hair and raised his other hand to point at her. "Tomorrow. My study. Meet at the same time."

"Yes, sir." She didn't understand him. Any other British master would not have cared about the welfare of one servant. She'd even heard of other generals encouraging their soldiers to beat their servants. How could he be so different? Then again, she'd never met another general who asked his servants about their opinions on the world.

To think she and Raj had assumed she would be a maid! She'd never separated one white man from another before; she'd viewed them all as treacherous. Raj had told her so many stories of how all generals were the same cold-hearted men who believed Indians to be inferior…would her brother believe her if she told him the man they worked for was different?

She took a deep breath and held her brother closer to her chest. One act of kindness didn't change who the general was or the institution his soldiers enforced. She was still a freedom fighter; he was still the enemy.

• • •

Colonel Curzon? No, too obvious. The grudge-holding Curzon had hated his guts ever since Warren called off Curzon's attack on the Indian village. That was nearly a year ago. If Curzon suspected he was a spy, he would have acted by now.

Colonel Leighworth? No, too spineless. Leighworth wouldn't hurt a fly. His troops barely respected him; there was no way he could gather enough courage to investigate covert activities of his superior officers.

Who else could have suspected his identity?

A sharp rap at the door interrupted his thoughts. The floorboards creaked beneath a veiled figure standing in the doorway.

"Ah, Miss Singh!" Warren picked up his fountain pen and shifted the paper on his desk closer to him. "Please sit down. Close the door behind you."

As soon as the door clicked shut, the girl removed her veil from around her head. The soft fabric gathered at the base of her shoulders. "What is it you wish to speak to me about?"

He shifted his weight in his seat. Time to try a new angle this time before she suspected it was an interrogation. "How is Raj?"

"Recovering." She looked down into her lap. "We cannot thank you enough for stepping in yesterday."

"Glad to hear it. Any rational man would do the same." He cleared his throat. "I assume your brother will be resting for a few days?"

"Today, yes." He watched her bite her bottom lip, then lift her widened eyes. "Though he wishes to return to his gardening duties as soon as possible."

"Give him time." So no anarchist activities for the time being. "How is your life at home?"

She arched an eyebrow. "Why do you ask?"

A politician's response, countering his question with one of her own. "I believe the soldiers yesterday said Raj called them his 'jailers,' correct? Is this a sentiment held by both you and your brother in your house, or singular to his perspective?"

"I believe my brother is only echoing sentiments he's heard within our village."

"How do the Indian villagers view the British colonization? I understand there have been several attempts at a noncooperative movement by Gandhi recently. *Swaraj*, I believe you call it…"

Her clipped tone cut him off. "Yes. We have no desire to be told how to run our own country."

"We?"

A blush swept across her cheeks. "The freedom fighters have no desire to be told. Not I."

He clucked his tongue. "Really? And how do *you* feel your country is being run by the British?"

"Inefficiently."

"In what ways?" His pen began to scribble over the piece of paper in front of him, noting her observations.

"Several of the railroads have caused misallocation of food and created famine. Indians are cut off from proper jobs and education, reduced to aspiring to be servants. We are given no say in how our government should be run."

He'd heard of her information before. Many of the British officers knew of the Deccan Riots…not that they cared to discuss the cause of such riots among themselves. The local farmers in western India had protested against rising taxes and farmers being forced to grow cotton. The cotton had been profitable, yet the plant had destroyed the soil and caused agricultural hardship. But that was nearly a generation ago. He hadn't realized that the British economic system still caused such harm. "Did you not have a caste system heavily imposed before we arrived?"

"Not all Hindustanis agreed with the caste system. Even then, we never committed deliberate violence against members of the lowest class, such as the British do to us. The racial superiority is worst. We are told that we matter less in this world simply because we are Indian."

He paused his writing. "Surely most Indians do not agree."

"No, we do not; many of us wish to fight for a new government. We fight for basic liberties."

A government? Not a system of anarchy? "The British government is not so terrible."

"And the Rowlatt Act was not?"

He set down his pen. The act had allowed the British government to imprison anyone suspected of terrorism in the Raj without a fair trial. In his opinion, it hadn't been too different from Roosevelt's crackdown on anarchists. He'd read that the Rowlatt Act had been so unpopular in India that even the British couldn't deny it. "The act's been repealed."

"Yet it was still imposed." He watched her eyes narrow. "As are all the other laws the British Raj puts in place."

"Self-rule takes time. What is so urgent about replacing one form of government for another?"

"One cannot replace lentils with stones. Even your British government cannot ignore the better political representation my Hindustanis can…" The flow of her words stopped, as if a wooden cork had prevented the words from overflowing. Her downcast gaze flicked up to meet his. "You wish to know about the details of our rebellion."

He bit back a laugh. The woman was good. "It is difficult to believe you were never formally educated, Miss Singh. Your vocabulary is impeccable."

"Do not change the subject, sir." Her tone was scathing. "Is it our rebellion you wish to know the details of?"

"Possibly." He nodded. "Not that your rebellion is much worry to speak of thus far."

"I would not say so, sir. I would say it should cause you much worry."

He'd never seen eyes as expressive as Parineeta's. They were full of questions and intelligence, yet there was something furtive about her glance at the same time. It was as if no matter how much information she shared with him, there was always something she held back.

"I have heard there are several revolutionaries living in the nearby villages."

She sniffed. "I know nothing of it."

A response too quick to be truth.

Warren gritted his teeth. He'd spent enough time as an operative to know when a woman was telling a lie. "I believe you do know, Miss Singh."

"I assure you that I do not."

He rubbed his jaw and swallowed down his frustration. Their conversation was starting to run in circles, tracing the same path and arriving nowhere significant. He had not invested a year undercover only to return empty-handed. So she wouldn't answer him directly, would she? Maybe not in so interrogative a setting.

Warren glanced around his office. The steel filing cabinets behind Parineeta loomed over her head. Diplomas and trophies the NBCI had supplied him with lined the many oak shelves, adding an aura of authority and intimidation to the room. Even if inauthentic, the memorabilia likely did nothing to calm her nerves. Maybe all she needed was a less pressuring environment.

A look of wariness filled her eyes and her shoulders stiffened. She certainly wasn't going to admit anything about the Indian revolutionaries now. He needed her trust. His fingers drummed against the table. *She's the best information source about Raj that I'll be able to find.* He had to find a way for her to open up to him.

"I appreciate you being able to speak with me so candidly," Warren backpedaled. He wracked his brain, searching for an opportunity. "Perhaps we can talk again tonight."

"Tonight?" Her lips pressed into a fine line. If her words had flowed like water down a river before, they were as rare as dry ground during the monsoon now. "I do not think so."

He chuckled. "No, no, nothing of that sort. I am organizing a small gathering for some guests tonight in my ballroom. I would love for you to attend."

"A party?" She shook her head. Dark tendrils that she'd gathered behind her shoulders fell forward, framing her high cheekbones and curling around her chin. "You must be mistaken. I am a..."

A pregnant pause filled the air. Warren watched her gaze flicker to her lap once more, as if confirming her skin color. A what, he wondered. A half-caste? An Indian?

She cleared her throat. "I would not be welcome."

"It is my party, after all. It is a chance to meet some other people in the region." *And a chance to try to figure out who knows my identity.* "You must come. I will introduce you as a woman who is helping me with my research."

"A half-Indian maid assisting you with research?"

The idea did sound better in his head. But what other choice did he have? "I want you to trust me, Parineeta." Before he could stop himself, her name rolled off his tongue like honey. He studied her expression as he spoke, hoping the look of fear would melt away. "I must insist. You are not just a maid. You are helping me with a very important project of mine."

She opened her mouth to protest. Doubt warred across her conflicted expression for a moment. Then she nodded. "Yes. Yes, I will go."

"Then it's settled! You'll be there tonight." His heart lifted as he clapped his hands. The brass buttons at the edge of his sleeve cuffs clinked together. "That is all for today. You may leave now."

"We have finished for the day so quickly?"

"It seems we have." Maybe he could bribe her to trust him. Who didn't like shortened tasks? "Considering you will be spending a few extra hours at my party tonight, I would say your day's work will still be the same as normal."

Parineeta raised an eyebrow. If she suspected anything, she didn't voice her suspicions. The ends of her skirt dragged across the floorboards as she stood up from her chair. Golden bangles clinked down her wrists as she opened the door and left the room.

As soon as the door closed, Warren stood from his own chair. This girl expected him to believe she knew nothing of the independence movement? He would have sooner believed Calvin Coolidge was the Queen of England!

He waited for her to stroll to the end of the hall before he followed after her. His leather shoes fell against the marble tile as quietly as he could manage, but her bare feet slapped against the tile and hurried away so fast that he doubted she would hear him even if he ran behind her.

He traced her path out the door, down the winding walkway, past the gardens, and across the dirt road leading away from the gates of his house. She headed toward a cluster of houses next to the gardens, right before the gate entrance, where some of the gardeners lived and a few of the soldiers went to smoke. He'd seen his soldiers hanging around the area a few times after drills, but he'd never seen a woman there before.

He ducked behind a tree as soon as he saw her stop. He leaned his head out from behind the trunk to watch her figure. She stood in place for a few moments, scanning the houses before her. Warren cautiously stepped forward. A large twig snapped beneath his right shoe. *Damn.* He whipped his head back behind the tree and waited for his breath to even out. It had been a while since he'd had to do field work.

He waited a few seconds and then risked looking back again. She was walking to the end of one of the white walls, where she knocked on a door three times.

Warren ducked behind another tree, closer to the door. Next to the new cluster of trees, she would not be able to see him…but he was within perfect earshot of whatever she uttered.

25

A creak could be heard from behind the corner. "Parineeta!"

Hold on, I recognize that voice. It was the gardener, wasn't it? The Indian his men had been beating yesterday. He leaned closer against the tree, craning his neck to hear more.

"What does he think of the HRA? What information have you learned?"

Information?

"I have only been spying on him for two days, Raj. I do not know much."

Warren frowned. He'd suspected she was a revolutionary, but he hadn't realized she'd been spying on him. The wisps of green plants before him, one of the few spots of color across the barren desert, swayed to the sound of her voice.

Perhaps she was his own spot of color. Who possessed more useful information about the revolutionaries than another spy?

• • •

"Yes, but two days is still a long while!"

Parineeta tapped her foot. She tried to peer beyond Raj's shoulder and into the garden shed he sometimes occupied. "Can you not let me in?"

"No, another gardener is sleeping in here." Raj's smile told her the person in his shed was no gardener. She shuddered.

"Look, I do not care who she is; just listen to me." Parineeta leaned forward. She attempted to keep her voice even. Now was not the time to worry him more than necessary. "I have been invited to the general's party tonight at his house."

"What?" Then he winced. After a hasty glance behind him at whoever was sleeping, he turned back to Parineeta. He kept his voice low. "Why would he invite you?"

"That is what I do not understand." She smoothed out the folds in her sari. The motion gave her a sense of comfort, unlike her current task. "This mission does not make any sense. He tells me that my information is essential to his project. He's asking me about the independence movement; he says I need to help him with his research…"

Raj's voice became cold. "You haven't given him any reason to know you're spying on him, have you? You do not want him to question your loyalties."

"No! Of course I wouldn't." She gulped. *At least I hope not.*

"Good." He pressed his lips together. "Then you should go tonight. See if you can find out any plans of how the British army is going to deal with my group. We'll take him down. Just wait."

Take him down? Her heartbeat quickened at the loaded threat. Parineeta's eyes drifted to the pocket in Raj's white trousers where she knew he kept his gun. When she was younger, she never understood why he even had the weapon. Even after beatings from other soldiers, he'd never pulled out his revolver. Not yet, anyway.

"Promise me you won't hurt him."

He scowled. "Why do you care?"

"He saved your life yesterday!"

"I was fine." Her brother looked away. His hand rested on his gun.

Parineeta folded her arms over her chest. "Let us not rush anything. I do not think this general is the same as all the other cruel ones we've known." Her memories jumped back to when her grandfather had still been alive. The past general had forced farmers to grow a crop that failed in their fields and still imposed the annual land tax that year, causing the entire village to suffer from famine. Her grandfather had given all the food they could afford to her grandmother, her mother, Raj, and herself. He'd died of starvation by the end of the winter. "But General Carton has been nothing but nice toward me."

"Nice enough for you to be deceived by him?"

She nearly slapped Raj across the cheek. The nerves in her palm twitched at the imagined contact. "That's enough, brother." She could hardly believe this gun-slinging revolutionary was the same brother who helped her with the laundry and made her *palak paneer* for dinner when her mother was working in the previous general's house. He'd seemed so innocent then. "I am nothing but loyal to the independence movement."

"Good." Raj shook his finger at her. "First rule—don't get caught. If you get caught, they'll find out about me. And then our whole village back home. They'll hurt our grandmother. Second rule—do not start to care for your boss."

Her cheeks burned. "What?"

"You are his servant. He would never care for you."

"I do not find him attractive." She whisked the thoughts of a blue-eyed, brown-haired general out of her mind. Her brother would find more comfort in her lies. "I learned from our mother that you can never trust men."

"You can trust me." Raj puffed out his chest. *How can he look so determined? He has no experience with fighting.* He took so much of the independence movement upon himself. "I'm heading out with Dev in a train robbery soon."

She narrowed her eyes. "I am coming with you."

"It is not safe for you. You should stay here."

Always with the overprotection. "What experience do you have with fighting?"

"My dedication is what matters, not my experience."

Her thin bangles chimed as she placed one hand on her hip. "You cannot get rid of me so easily. I am as dedicated to this movement as you are."

Her brother turned his attention away from her. He craned his neck toward the road behind her and looked over her shoulder. "What was that?"

Parineeta frowned. "What are you talking about?"

He held a finger up to his lips and cupped one tanned hand behind his ear. "I just heard someone."

"It's probably the wind." She looked up at the threatening sky. The summer rains were as unpredictable as the general's requests. Heavy rain could fall any day now or maybe not for another two weeks. "Or the roll of the incoming monsoon. That is all."

He nodded but still scanned the road behind her shoulder with a wary eye. "You should be careful as well. You never can trust the British."

Chapter Four

You never could trust the British. One moment you felt sure you were accepted as one of them, and the next moment you received a letter saying they've found out about your secret identity. He bent his head back to finish the rest of the pale Scotch in his crystal glass. Trust the British, indeed.

"I said, this is *my new fiancée.*"

Warren looked away from the fireplace to the woman standing before him. Ah, Shelly Hastings. And a simpering, slouching man in a starched collar next to her.

"How do you do?" He set his empty glass down on the mantel and shook the man's hand. His large palm enveloped the smaller man's clammy hand. "I hope you and Miss Hastings are well."

Shelly cleared her throat. "Lloyd and I were thinking of a spring wedding." She narrowed her emerald-green eyes at Warren. "You always loved the idea of a spring wedding, didn't you?"

He resisted the urge to groan. Agree with a woman once and she reminded you forever. Shelly Hastings would never forgive him, would she? He hadn't even realized she'd been flirting with him until she'd already started babbling on to all the other officers about their supposed wedding details. "That was some time ago, Miss Hastings."

Shelly huffed in indignation. "Not so long. Just a season, I think." The turquoise silk of her dress strained against her figure as she wrapped her arm around the simpering sod's. "Lloyd and I are much better suited, though, I do believe. Don't you, Lloyd?"

Lloyd grunted. He didn't seem to have much of an opinion on the matter.

She smiled. "See? He and I are well-suited."

"I wish you two all the happiness in the world." Warren managed to force a small smile for her sake.

Shelly batted her thick lashes at him as a self-satisfied smirk crossed her features. Her blond curls bounced against her shoulders as she gestured to the other side of the ballroom. "Do not despair, General Carton. Someday you will find your own domestic bliss. Lloyd and I must say hello to Lady Lanister, if you'll excuse us."

Warren watched her walk away with her fiancée's arm in tow. God bless him. Shelly was lovely to look at; there was no real reason he hadn't been able to marry her. A general should be married, or so all the other ladies loved to remind him. Shelly especially.

He turned his gaze back to the fireplace, where he knew the ashes of the cryptic letter remained. Where was the time for love in a profession such as his? How could he allow himself to settle with a woman when he knew he would have to leave her in a few years when his assignment ended?

Not that he'd remained very long in the current one. And who was he supposed to report to now—the National Bureau of Criminal Identification or the Federal Bureau of Investigation? His gaze flickered between the different generals present. Brass buttons shined to perfection beneath the light of the hanging chandelier. Half the uniformed men tolerated him, and the other half were all plotting to become viceroy and surpass him. Any other powerful officer was a threat.

Warren bit back a bitter smile. He was no threat to professional success. Just an agent passing through, looking for some answers and a mission to complete. Speaking of a completed mission… where was the vital instrument to his?

He scanned the crowd for a sight of her tan skin and curled mane. Crepe dresses in pastel colors swayed across the floor, their reflections bouncing off the mirrors on the upper half of each wall. Gentlemen in suits escorted women with finger wave hairstyles from the sidelines to the center of the ballroom. All the ladies were either plump wives of British generals or their innocent daughters.

The same fair hair, fairer skin, and delicate steps as dainty as they were demure.

Several of the women met his gaze, fluttering their lashes in what Warren suspected was a half-hearted attempt to capture his attention. His eyes shifted to each one, searching for the Anglo-Indian beauty with fiery responses and unabashed opinions. He expected a swish of bright sari to come sweeping through the crowd at any moment, pushing aside the sea of pearls and silk tulle dresses with the beat of her bangles.

Yet she was nowhere to be seen. Not in the mass of starched tuxedos and lace evening dresses, anyway. Where was Parineeta?

He walked into the long hallway, past the party guests and beyond the violinists and even further than the swirling dresses and shining brass buttons of the dancing couples. His footsteps quickened as worry settled in his gut. Maybe she'd decided not to show up.

He'd given specific instructions to the maid to have her ready hours ago. There was no chance she would still be waiting next to the...

"Parineeta?"

The slender figure rested one delicate hand over the polished staircase railing. She'd placed one foot onto the first marble step of the winding staircase. Her back was facing him, and her position was frozen in place. Yet her torso remained twisted to the side, as if he'd caught her in a sudden movement to run away from the crowd.

"Where are you going?"

"I cannot go out there." She lowered her foot and placed the slipper back onto the ground. The draped silk fabric of her black evening gown brushed against the floor as she stepped down, contrasting against the white marble tile.

He could hear her voice tremble. How strange that a girl who seemed so spirited and full of passion for independence could feel so insecure before facing the men she proposed to fight. Surely it wasn't about her appearance. She was prettier than all of the other women in the room.

"And why is that?"

"They will recognize me." Her voice sounded tight. "They will know I am half-caste. I am not one of them."

The music from the other end of the hall drifted along the corridors and played softly around the stairwell, the once lively rhythm settling into a mellower tune. He straightened the front of his shirt. "What is the matter with that?"

Parineeta's voice gained strength. Irritation crept into her tone. She turned to the side, half of her face exposed to the light. "You would not understand."

"Maybe I would, maybe I wouldn't. That does not mean you shouldn't come out here." Warren started forward.

All he could see with her back turned to him was her black dress. The gown covered her shoulders, and long, lace gloves fitted over her hands and wrists. There was even a beaded cloche hat placed on the top of her head.

"I am sure you look fine." He struggled to keep the exasperation out of his voice. He stepped closer again and drummed his fingers against the wooden railing next to him. "I told the maids to spare no expense on buying you clothes for tonight."

He watched her shoulders rise and fall with a sudden intake of breath. "You should not have done that."

Warren smirked. "Most women would say thank you."

"I am not most women."

"Clearly."

She sighed. "I look nothing like myself."

"Let me see."

She turned slowly at first, with a hesitating step, and then with a swish of her gown she stood directly in front of him.

Warren's jaw dropped.

Good lord…

Her natural beauty hadn't been altered by her attire. It was still there, the golden perfection of her skin and the intense gaze of her eyes. But the woman in front of him looked nothing like the bangle-wearing, veil-covered girl his gardener had presented to him a few days ago. This woman had her naturally wavy hair brushed into an up-do, a string of pearls around her neck, and shining jeweled earrings placed on her lobes. The light of the chandelier above them illuminated the light brown highlights in her otherwise black tresses, while the silver accents of the sides of her black dress sparkled against her creamy skin. She looked beautiful.

"I look bad."

Warren blinked. "What?" He blinked several more times, trying to register the sight in front of him. "What did you say?"

"I look terrible."

"No, no, you look…" He searched for the right words. His entire vocabulary suddenly fled his memory at that moment, leaving him at a loss. All he could do was shake his head like a dumb mule. "You look…"

"Ridiculous and out of place, I am aware." She pulled at her left earlobe, fiddling with the diamond-encrusted earring. "These clothes are not very comfortable."

"You look amazing."

The thin lining of kohl framing Parineeta's eyes made her bright expression appear even braver. She arched one full brow at him. "Is that so, sir?"

"Call me Warren tonight." He lifted the cuffed white sleeve of his coat, offering his arm to her. "You are my research assistant, and I am your employer. That is all we are for tonight."

She slipped her glove-covered arm around his. A loose tendril of wavy black hair grazed the top of her right cheekbone as she regarded him with suspicion. "Why are you doing all this for me?"

"I have my reasons." Warren guided her into the bustling ballroom full of British generals and their wives. "Just as you have yours." He felt her arm stiffen around his at the last sentence.

Now was not the time to be distracted, especially by another spy, no matter what beauty she may have been hiding. His shallow breath filled the quiet corridor.

He pressed his hand into the small of her back. She arched at the movement, the soft black fabric beneath his hands slipping out of reach at the sudden contact. There was a certain elegance to her movements, a lightness of step he had at first attributed to the sway of her sari. But even in the evening dress she retained the same poise, her slim shoulders pressed back as the curve of her hips shifted from side to side.

The chandelier threw light against the walls, reflecting across the several gold-leafed mirrors and directly along the center of the floor as the pair entered the room. As he and Parineeta slowed to a halt, a hush descended over the crowd. All eyes turned to Parineeta as his hand fell from her back. Her arm gripped his tighter, and he winced.

"There's no need to worry," he whispered.

Or so he hoped.

The elder women at the party had already started fanning themselves, disguising their scowls of Old World disapproval beneath their white ostrich feather fans. The younger ladies took more brazen approaches to the sight, some openly gawking with their jaws wide open while others pointed.

Among these spectators, he spotted Shelly's mop of blond curls out of the corner of his eye. If her whispers to Lloyd were supposed to be private, she wasn't doing a tremendous job of keeping quiet. "Who's that girl?"

In truth, he could barely answer the question himself.

"General Carton!" A young colonel strolled up to Warren. His breath smelled of whiskey, but his smile remained harmless. "How are you and your lady?"

A weight lifted off Warren's chest. He'd always liked Colonel Williams. The man refused to use punishment on his Indian servants, and he was known for paying his employees more than other British masters in the area. He was also, thankfully, much less judgmental than the other generals. "Fine, just fine. May I introduce my research assistant, Parineeta Singh?"

"A research assistant? Whatever for?"

The voice sounded cold and clipped. Definitely not from the colonel. Warren turned to the source and resisted the urge to groan. Lieutenant Colonel Ellington.

"What are you doing, cavorting with a coolie?" Ellington practically spat the words into Warren's face. His wrinkled forehead pressed into a map of thin lines and crow's feet as he peered at the couple.

Warren kept his tone even. The whiskey from earlier in the evening began to warm his cheeks, and a flash of annoyance flared through him. "Your remarks are unwelcome by everyone, Ellington. This woman has a name; I suggest you use it."

"I will not learn the name of a half-caste wastrel," the old man said. He laughed, the hollow sound empty and mocking. "You must have fallen upon hard times indeed if you must turn to the other race."

"Race does not matter in this house," he managed to reply through gritted teeth.

The half-balding man's eyes gleamed with a spark of something sinister. "But then again, you can afford to throw your career away now."

Warren's stomach plummeted. *Your identity has been compromised*...of course it was Ellington! The ambitious lieutenant colonel had pined for the position of general since the moment he first stepped foot in India. There was every reason for him to keep tabs on all the generals, including Warren.

"What are you referring to, Ellington?"

"I think you know what *correspondence* I speak of."

Warren resisted the urge to curse aloud. The damned letters! He knew he should have burned all of them from the beginning. He hadn't been able to keep track of every missive passing between him and the chief of the Bureau of Identification. If someone had found one of them and learned shorthand, he would be able to decipher them.

Ellington sneered. "So sorry to ruin your little party." Then the lieutenant colonel turned to the other guests. "Everyone! Everyone, I would like your attention, please!"

Warren's eyes widened. No time to waste. Adrenaline rushed through his veins as he released Parineeta's arm. At her quizzical look, he leaned to whisper in her ear, "I'll be in the front of the house, near the gates. I will see you in a minute."

Ellington had stepped too far forward on the floor to see Warren, who used the opportunity to slip away from the front of the room.

The moment his right foot crossed the threshold between the hallway and the ballroom, a small hand tugged his arm back. He jerked at the hold, but the grip only tightened. Before he could shove his captor away, he found himself face to face once more with Parineeta.

"There's no reason for you to leave." She wrinkled her nose. "This is your party."

"This won't be my party anymore in a few minutes."

"What are you talking about?

"I'll explain later. Meet me in the front." It would be easier for both of them to slip away unnoticed if they left separately. Without waiting for her reply, he pushed past her. Her hold loosened, and she allowed him to leave without uttering another word.

His footsteps raced down the hall, as far as possible from the rest of the group. The cooler air of the corridors rushed against his back once he picked up his stride. His escape stood only a few yards away, an arched doorway highlighting the Indian desert beyond the safety of his walls.

Not that there's much safety for me here now. The sight of such unknown terrain provided no welcome relief to his soul. He sighed as he ran a hand through his close-cropped hair. If things went the way Ellington wanted, Parineeta would have her explanation soon enough.

• • •

"Ladies and gentlemen, may I please have your attention? I have a grave admittance to make that concerns everyone in this room."

Parineeta looked behind her shoulder. Warren was gone; he would miss the important announcement. Her arm felt strangely bare without his own arm wrapped around hers. What had made him slip away so suddenly?

Her cheeks burned as she thought of his request. It was hardly decent to ask a girl he'd just met to meet him in the dark in secret. She risked her reputation enough by agreeing to spend so much time alone with him in his office already. If he thought she was going after him, he must be mad.

"I would like to inform all of you…"

She frowned. But why would Warren leave in such a hurry? Was she in danger here and that was why she needed to meet him? She interlaced her fingers at the front of her dress. The silk gown rustled beneath her movement. Whatever this tiny bald man wished to say, she wished he'd make the news quick.

"…that we have a spy in our midst!"

Parineeta swore her heartbeat halted for several moments. She covered her mouth with one long, black glove and bit her lower lip before any words could leave her lips. How could anyone have known about her mission at the general's house? The hairs on the back of her neck stood up.

"Are you mad, George?" Another one of the generals waved his silver cup in the air. "We're all friends here. Don't be ridiculous! How could there be a spy?"

"You do not seem to know everyone quite as much as you've assumed. The man we all know as General Carton is actually an American spy!"

The woman standing next to him gasped. A few frightened looks from the guests were thrown about the room.

Parineeta would have rolled her eyes at the theatrics if she were not so alarmed. She kept the glove over her mouth. An outburst from her would help no one. The general could not be a spy. The notion was even more outlandish than the idea of milking goats in her current gown.

Whispers of scandal drifted through the guests. The short man who'd made the first announcement lowered his spectacles further down the bridge of his nose. His black, beady eyes scanned the crowd before him. "Where is this traitor? Bring him up here!"

"What proof do you have?" A tall woman with curly, blond hair tossed her mane back behind her frilly sleeves and scoffed. "General Carton is a respectable leader in the British Raj. I highly doubt you can prove your claims."

"Letters! I have intercepted letters!" The man passed numerous papers to different members of his audience. Those in the crowd murmured among themselves upon reading each piece of paper, each one passing along the folded letters with traumatized looks on their faces.

The man stamped his foot against the marble floor. He looked like a child, waving his arms like a lunatic and barking commands with impatience. "I said bring him to me! Who was with him?

Who last saw him?" Parineeta couldn't help but think of the village drunk who did little more than shout at others.

The only difference between this man and the village drunk was that this small man had an entire troop of Indian and British soldiers at his command. The village drunk could throw broken bottles at his targets from time to time but never armed mercenaries.

Parineeta stepped away from the crowd, her slippers edging backward inch by inch until she bumped into a cold wall. Her heartbeat drummed in her ears. She rubbed her palms against the front of her dress. Only one word echoed in her mind: *escape.*

She turned her cheek to the ballroom and raced down the corridor. The long, draping material of the silk dress swished behind her. The warmth of the summer night air wrapped around her arms like a shawl, cloaking her in much needed darkness. She darted out the doorway between the marble columns and dashed down the wooden steps, along the narrow road and toward her safe home.

She was jerked back as a large hand reached out to grab her wrist. The muscular grip behind the tree remained firm as she tugged her arm to wrench free from the hold.

"Stop! Just stop, please."

She stepped behind the tree, and the man dropped his hand. Her wrist stung. "Warren?"

"I told you to meet me here, didn't I?" He shoved his hands into his pockets and closed his eyes. The dark brown of his hair nearly disappeared into the trunk of the tree, while the harsh illumination of the moon's rays bathed him in critical light. He rested against the tree, one foot propped up against the bark while the other remained planted on the ground. "Glad you finally showed up."

She glanced past his shoulder to peek at the road leading out to the streets and her own village. The crickets chirped from the south, as if beckoning her home. Maybe it wasn't too late to escape…

He opened his eyes suddenly. One look from those clear ocean colored orbs and she found herself suddenly rooted to the spot.

"How did it go?"

"As you would expect." She placed both her gloved hands onto her hips. "I thought the man was lying at first."

"And now?"

Parineeta pressed her lips into a thin line. "Who are you?"

"I could ask you the same question."

He almost sounded amused. *Crazy man.* How anyone could act so nonchalant when his life was at stake, she could not understand. Her brows stitched together as she narrowed her eyes at him. "I am not the one hiding from my own party. What are you doing here?"

"What does it look like?" One hand emerged from his pocket to run it through his hair. The other remained shoved in the pocket of his pressed trousers. "I'm clearly going back to receive their award and bask in their thunderous applause in my honor."

"Your voice…it's…" Parineeta couldn't believe her ears. The natural British accent she'd grown accustomed to hearing was replaced by an even more natural American one. She drew in a quick intake of breath. "You are not from Britain."

"I should hope not. Pretty certain Ellington told everyone, though."

She blinked. So he really was a spy! "You're from America?"

"Raised there. Not born there."

Parineeta looked back toward the mansion. The twisting marble stairwell on the side of the house remained bare, and the second-floor balcony held no traces of a search party. No one had left the house yet, but she figured it was only a matter of time before they started looking for him outside. "How could you be a spy?"

"I could ask you the same question."

She shifted her weight from one foot to the other. This man's ability to see right through her secrets was unnerving. Oh, what would Raj do? Her firebrand of a brother would probably tell her to keep lying. "I have no idea what you are talking about."

Warren glanced behind the tree to risk another survey of the empty clearing outside his house and then gave her a pointed look. "Don't try to pull one over on me. I followed you and heard you talking to your brother."

Her right hand balled into a fist. She'd been foolish to leave his house so quickly and not expect an ulterior motive. "You had no such right."

"Really? And you had such a right to spy on me?"

Her cheeks felt hot. "It doesn't matter anymore." Parineeta jutted out her chin. "Not that being caught has changed anything. Clearly you have no useful information for me to report, nor do you have the ability to expose me."

"I wouldn't say that."

She interlaced her fingers together in front of her, the satin gloves sliding over each other. A cool wind brushed past her cheek, causing her to shiver. When a warm summer evening faded into a chilling windy night, it was never a good omen. "Why were you waiting for me?"

Warren grabbed her arm. "I'll explain later."

"No!"

"Let's go, Parineeta."

"Let go of me!" She yanked her arm away from his hold, and his hand fell back. He wanted to kidnap her! She had stayed too long in this lavish nightmare. Time to return home.

A sudden series of yells caught her attention. Before she could turn around to figure out the source of the sound, Warren held her chin in his hands and kept her gaze fixed on his.

"Just follow my lead. Trust me." His grip around her upper arm tightened, and they began to race away from the tree. Her feet flew across the ground at the same pace as his, but she had no idea where they were sprinting toward.

Before she could ask, she heard another roar behind her. Even while her strides remained in tandem with Warren's, she chanced a glance over her shoulder. Her throat became dry as she took in the sight.

The balcony was no longer empty. The entire crowd from the ballroom had gathered on the second floor to watch the drama unfold before their eyes. Below them, a legion of the British Raj's best generals and colonels streamed down the stairwell, headed straight in her direction. She could see other officers jumping onto horses in the background, while others who'd had an earlier start led the pack with their steeds.

"Know any good hiding spots?"

Parineeta guided him away from the dirt road and off the end of the paved path. She ran as fast as her feet would carry her as she led Warren further and further away from the road. He'd stopped trying to remain in step with her, instead choosing to follow her path, always a few steps behind. Her lungs began to constrict as she felt herself becoming winded, but every time she considered slowing down, she heard the stampede of footsteps behind them… or were they the harried gallops of hooves? Never had she been chased before, and the thought of capture was terrifying.

She winced as her ankle scraped against an upturned root. Pain flashed through her calf as she continued to place weight on the injured foot. Branches snapped beneath their weight as the cleared dirt started to give way to forest ground.

It wasn't until they were deep into the foliage that Parineeta finally stopped. She'd been here before as a child, playing with other village children. Yet the sight of so many Ashoka trees overhead had never seemed more ominous than when she noticed them by night. She cupped a hand around her ear and craned her neck to listen for any sounds behind them. No footsteps, no horse hooves. They were safe.

For now.

A clicking brought her attention back to the man before her. He was panting, his beige pants splotched with dark spots of dirt and his shirt untucked from his wide belt. He had pulled out two guns, holding them to his sides at the ready as he scanned the jungle around them. There was a crazed look in his eyes. He raised both his revolvers to the sky, as if in a stance to shoot whoever—or whatever—approached him.

All right, maybe she wasn't so safe.

"Put those down," she begged. "You have no use for them here."

He refused to make eye contact with her, his own gaze fixed on the dark foliage before him. His unsteady steps formed a small circle in the dirt. "Wild animals. They could attack."

Parineeta laughed. The fearsome man in disguise was afraid of nature. "I thought you were a trained spy."

"Spying in a cosmopolitan city and spying in the middle of nowhere are much different, I assure you."

"And this is no city. I think you were the one who needed my help to escape, not the other way around. What do you know of the jungle?"

Warren put the guns away, to her relief. He gave one last distrusting gaze to the trees surrounding him on all sides. "You're right. I don't know very much about it."

At least we agree on one matter. She bent down, resting her hands on the insides of her thighs and sucking pockets of air into her lungs like a man dying of thirst. "You have finally admitted my usefulness after all."

"Exactly. That's why you're going to guide me out of here and help me reach Lucknow."

Parineeta brought herself back up to her full height and folded her arms across her chest. He couldn't just order her around as he pleased. "I am not your servant anymore."

"Of course you are not my servant. But you must still help me." He started walking ahead of her, weaving his way in and out of the thicket of the bushes in a zigzag motion. She half expected him to start using the butt of his pistol as a scythe against the leaves.

Take him to Lucknow? Was he crazy? She pulled off the black gloves from her hands, sliding the constraining fabric off her wrists before she threw them on the forest floor. "What makes you think I would do that?"

"Because if you do…" He pushed aside a tree branch and looked back over his shoulder at her. "I'll give you any information you want."

"What?"

"Plans to strike down rebellions. Hidden armories. Places where the independence movement will find wealthy sympathizers willing to donate money. Names of the freedom fighters that the British government has their eye on."

Her heartbeat quickened. "And what the British Army thinks of the revolutionaries? What they think of the Hindustan Republican Association?"

"Yes and yes."

"But…you're not a real general." Parineeta bit her lower lip. Still, at least he had pretended to be one. Surely he must have picked up some useful information during that time. She smoothed a hand over her hair, fumbling with the pins and managing to release her tresses from the up-do. Her hat had fallen off during the chase as well. "How can I trust that you're telling me the truth?"

"And how can I trust you?" Warren started toward her, pointing an accusatory finger against her chest. "You're the one who spied on me first."

She puffed out her chest and stepped closer. The closing distance caused him to drop his hand. "You're the one who got caught. Of the two of us, you are the one in the worse position."

"Me? Do you really think Lieutenant Colonel Ellington won't question why an American *spy* was meeting with a 'research assistant'?"

She pressed her pointed index finger into his chest, agitation rising in her own. This man was determined to drive her crazy. "That's your fault for bringing me to your event. Do not make demands of me."

He inched closer to her until she could feel his hot breath upon her face. "You have a choice. Walk away now if you want."

"I said nothing about walking away." She swallowed hard as she noticed the quick rise and fall of his chest with each breath he took. His lips were so close that if she turned her head, her lips would brush his. Heat spread across the apples of her cheeks. "Your information would be helpful."

"I told you, it is yours." He leaned toward her. His breath was heavy, and his hands were clasped together before him. Speaking with him in his office and arguing with him about their survival were two entirely different matters. "You help me, and I will help you."

If he thought wielding weapons would be enough to take them to Lucknow, he was in for a surprise. She gave a small smile. "I believe there will be more of me helping you. How can I trust you will give me the information?"

"How can I trust that you will guide me to Lucknow?" He brushed back a stray lock of dark hair that had fallen across his forehead. There was little patience in his tone.

Many of the other generals were blond, fair-haired, and fat. Warren was different. While his complexion remained far fairer than hers, his dark brows and thick hair were striking. The height difference between them was such that if she stared directly ahead, she saw only his chiseled jaw and…

Parineeta tore her eyes away from his lips and drew away, bringing herself back to reality. In spite of the numerous tears at the end of her dress, she smoothed out the creases in her far-from-salvageable gown as if it were one of her own saris; she would look anywhere except that dangerous and demanding mouth of his.

She shook her head. This situation—this man!—was impossible. She undid the earring clasps and clenched her fists around the jewels. She could sell this jewelry later; her brother and his friends needed all the money they could get to fund their activities. "Can't you tell me the information first?"

"That's not how this arrangement works. First, lead us to Lucknow."

If she actually could pass along the information he had gathered from his mission, her brother could use the view to refocus his revolutionary group's efforts. In the early days, Raj hadn't even realized that the British Army was aware of the revolutionary activities of the villagers. She still remembered all the late nights her brother had stayed up planning armory raids, peering over elaborate maps and discussing escape routes…only to discover the armories were already depleted. He'd returned at such late hours with nothing but a defeated expression and a voice full of disappointment.

She sighed, feeling a wave of defeat wash over her. "Why do you need to go to Lucknow?"

"That is for me to know and you to find out on your own, *pagal ladki*."

"Crazy girl?" Parineeta scoffed. Of course, he would only know insulting Hindi phrases.

He stepped around her, ignoring her words as he pushed his way into the jungle.

How dare he force her into such situations! She scowled at his retreating figure. "Who's the one who will guide us both? I am not crazy!"

"Then prove it to me by getting me out of this godforsaken jungle," he replied over his shoulder.

Parineeta narrowed her eyes but continued after him. She hardly had a choice. Return back to her brother with a failed mission and live with the guilt of losing an opportunity to serve her country…or guide this crazy American to Lucknow.

Bhagwan, of all the madmen to be trapped with!

Chapter Five

"I'm not so bad, am I?"

"Ravana, the ten-headed king, did not seem so bad. Then he kidnapped Sita and forced Rama to go into exile."

He scratched his chin. He'd heard the epic tale of Rama and Sita once before. Rama was an avatar of the Hindu god Vishnu, and his wife had been named Sita. Hold on, hadn't Ravana been the king of demons?

Instead of clarifying which story hero he possibly was, she lifted her cupped hands to her lips and drank the water that pooled in the small crevice. Warren turned away and stretched, scanning the bay, where small fishing boats were tied to even more antiquated wooden posts, swaying next to the dock and creating ripples in the water. A light patter of rain fell onto the floating vessels, filling them slowly.

He craned his neck. Sleeping on jungle ground for the past few days hadn't been safe, but it sure seemed a lot better than being captured by British hands. The monsoon air hung over their heads, sticky and inescapable. His hand swatted at a fly buzzing at the back of his neck, his palm running against the beads of sweat on his upper back in the process.

How to return to America? He'd heard of the activities of the Indian National Congress, but he somehow doubted the nationalist organization would assist an agent sent to collect fingerprints of the Indian anarchists. The rules that the NBCI had given him were simple: create Bertillon records, jot down some notes, determine how much Raj Singh's anarchist influence might influence the United States, then find another agent to pass along the documents and get the hell out.

Not that the government wanted any civilians to know that the US feared global influences. Last he'd heard, everyone was convinced that the bureau was just a domestic organization. In truth, he was certain that the US would prefer to end any international threat that could influence Americans.

He patted his left pocket. Crumpled notes of information on Raj Singh were tucked away, ready to be sent to the United States. But what if those weren't the rules of the FBI? Would this new organization that the NBCI had folded into want him to stay? He groaned in frustration. No point in questioning. First, find the other agent in Lucknow.

He turned his head to address Parineeta. "How far is the walk from here?"

"You cannot walk all the way. Soon we will travel by train."

He thrust his right hand into an empty pocket. "We have no money."

"The passage will be free."

"Free?" Perhaps the heat was getting to him. He wiped off the sweat dripping from the side of his forehead with the back of his shirt sleeve. He'd abandoned his coat and tie long ago in favor of the white shirt he wore underneath.

"I know some of the passengers." She paused. "They will be willing to pay for us."

"I guess you already know other people headed to Lucknow, then. Who do you know on the train?"

"My brother and his friends." Parineeta picked up the clay pot back on the dock and filled the container. She'd changed back into a traditional sari once they'd reached the nearby market. She'd also been the one to buy their food and drink after Warren had made the mistake of accompanying her into a market in a previous village. He hadn't realized it was possible to catch the judgmental attention of so many strangers until that day.

"Your brother?" He raised a brow. *Why would that anarchist be headed to Lucknow?*

She smirked.

That's not an answer. Still, he figured it was better not to press the issue. He was at the mercy of wherever this enchanting former spy guided him. No use in denying a free ride, no matter how it came about. And they weren't accomplishing anything standing around like this, even if his stiff joints protested in movement this morning.

He walked toward her, the muscles in his legs stretching with the strain. His limbs could use a lift by locomotive. He'd grown accustomed to riding horses, and he'd gained experience driving cars…walking for long distances was an entirely different story.

"So then you agree to take the train?"

Worry tied Warren's stomach in knots. "What? What's so funny?"

She tucked a stray lock of brown hair back into her thick braid, winding down one side of her shoulder and peeking out of her sari. "This is no ordinary train ride."

"I know, we're running from British soldiers." He wished she'd stop looking so damn amused for no reason. The sight was even more unsettling than the strange looks he received in the village. He'd been surprised at how adept she had been in knowing where to go; even with a blasted map he wouldn't have been able to cover this much ground on his own. If someone were racking up a debt between them, he was much more indebted to her.

Parineeta's smirk widened into a grin. She was the one with power now, not him. "We are going to join my brother's train robbery."

• • •

"We need to make our fire earlier next time. It's not safe to be on the move this late."

"Perhaps if you had gathered more firewood like I asked of you…" Who would have thought pretend generals would be so bossy even after their covers were blown?

"I know how to construct an automobile from spare parts, I can fluently speak and read thirteen languages, I am trained in seven different kinds of martial arts forms…"

"…but you do not know how to build a fire in this jungle," Parineeta finished. "And you do not know the proper price when haggling for samosas. And you do not know which way it is to Lucknow."

Warren's shoulders slumped. "They don't teach you those things during training."

"It seems my upbringing has made me better prepared for your mission than you are." It was almost endearing, how much he tried to make himself seem useful for their journey. She stoked the fire, poking the medium-sized stick into the flames. The fire was fine; she just found herself enjoying teasing this man. It was the least torture she could inflict upon him, considering the ultimatum he'd given her a few days before, though he had agreed to help in the robbery. She hadn't expected him to agree as soon as he had. She pushed her braid away from her collarbone and out of the fire's way. *Unless he had changed his mind.*

"You are still willing to help in the train robbery, you said?"

Warren shrugged. "Do I have a choice?"

"Not if you want to be in Lucknow before the British find you," she quipped. She pursed her lips. "But you seem willing."

"Maybe I am."

She resisted the urge to roll her eyes. Instead, she set down the stick she had been using to stoke the fire on a nearby rock. "We can stop with the mysteries now."

He snorted. "We? I hide nothing. You are the one who remains a mystery."

She stared into the fire, watching the amber flames dance before her eyes without focusing on anything in particular. Crickets chirped in the background while the firewood singed and crackled under the orange heat. How annoying. This man could tell when she still possessed secrets to keep. "How am I a mystery?"

"How did you become involved in the independence movement?"

She looked up from the flames and directly into Warren's gaze. He'd taken off his button-up shirt in the heat of the day; his skin seemed more bronzed by firelight. She wished he'd kept on his evening wear for the party. If not for the flames between them blocking the image of his chest, Parineeta would have surely looked away. "Why are you so curious about the revolutionaries?"

"See what I mean? I know nothing about you." Warren threw up his hands. "You're more of a mystery than me."

"No." She glanced at the foliage behind him. The large, flat leaves of the jungle trees covered them on all sides, shielding their forms—and the fire, she hoped—from prying eyes. For the moment, she felt safe.

"Let me guess: Is it another secret you don't want me to know?"

She sighed. It would be hours until dawn. There was no other way to pass the time than answer the pestering questions. Perhaps if she satisfied his fleeting curiosity, he would trust her with more information. "My brother was the first in my family to be involved with the revolutionaries. He told me about Gandhi's noncooperation movement. Then he and his friends from another village joined another independence group."

"How does one become involved in this group, anyway?" He stood up and stretched his arms above him. The hard muscles of his bare chest gleamed by the flames. She resented the way her heart raced at the sight. Too distracting. Couldn't he put on a shirt? Or at least a scarf around his neck to cover his chest, like the other men in her village did. Even a vest would have been fine.

She tried to concentrate on the heat from the flame and not the heat emanating from her cheeks. She'd seen plenty of shirtless men laboring in the fields before. None of the rest had ever caused her lips to pucker and her palms to perspire. "Word of mouth."

Warren sat next to her. She could feel the intensity of his eyes upon her. "But surely there must have been some event or some idea that triggered everyone to begin meeting."

"It's all just a matter of who understands and who doesn't." The crackle of the flames was interrupted by the low baying of a wolf somewhere far off behind her. Goosebumps rose on her arm. Even a warm fire couldn't protect someone from the world. *Nowhere was safe*, the wolf seemed to say.

"Understands what?"

"The Jallianwala Bagh massacre." A lump rose in her throat. Parineeta swore she heard the screams of the fallen in her head as she gazed into the fire. "A peaceful group of men, women, and children met to protest the arrest of two community leaders. They went against the recent rule of a curfew for all Indians. A general ordered his soldiers to fire onto the crowd." She bit her lip until she tasted blood. "None were armed. They had no way of escaping or fighting back."

Silence descended between the two for several seconds.

"I cannot even imagine."

She felt a lump form within her throat. "Sometimes I can. Hindustanis of all different ages. Grandmothers and babies. None were spared. The soldiers cornered them against walls and gates and shot at them." Her voice cracked, in spite of how hard she sought to control her tone. "Some jumped into wells." She heard the cries of women and children as they splashed into watery depths, favoring death by drowning over death by bullets. She could see the desperate few who remained alive clinging to the metal gates, begging those outside to open up until they, too, became riddled with bullets. She heard the cry of her own mother.

It wasn't until Warren had placed one hand over hers that she realized she'd been clutching at her sari skirt. She jerked her hands away, releasing the crumpled fabric.

"The reports say 370 died," he said softly.

Parineeta glared at him. As much he could try to empathize, he would never understand. His perspective was too clouded by privilege. "Your reports are wrong. Locals say close to 1,000 people died that day." She swallowed hard as she wiped away the tears welling up in her eyes. *No.* She would not cry in front of him. "My mother was visiting a friend in Amritsar at the time of the massacre. She never came home."

Whenever she tried to picture what happened, she always imagined her mother in different positions, in one vision running toward the gates until a bullet gunned her in the back, in another vision leaping into a well and drowning at the bottom, in another… She couldn't hold back anymore. The dam broke, causing tear-stained paths to stream down her cheeks. "Do your people not see us as humans?"

"I heard that the brigadier general who gave the orders didn't know that Jallianwala Bagh was in a closed space. He thought the protestors would be able to leave."

And outrun bullets aimed at their backs? "Oh, yes, now it makes everything so much more understandable to know he opened fire in an area he knew little about." She swallowed hard. "Are we worth so little that we can be shot down for no reason?"

Warren brushed his thumb against her cheek, swiping at the trail of tears. His soft touch contrasted the tightness in his voice. "You're worth ten times the lot of them. And I'm sure your mother was, too. The brigadier general who gave the command was removed from India."

"And…will that resurrect my mother? Or the lives of the others who perished that day?"

"Of course not." He stroked the top of her hair. "None of those people deserved their fate."

"I don't believe in fate." She laughed, hollow and bitter. How many times had she blamed herself for what happened? If only she'd prevented her mother from visiting Amritsar, if only she hadn't told her mother about how much she believed in the power of protesting. But none of the guilt would change anything. She could only try to stop such an event from happening again. "I believe in revenge. But don't worry." Parineeta clasped her hands together in her lap and looked down at her laced fingers. "This is not your fight."

"It will be when I step on that train."

She smiled at his readiness to accept the challenge. "Not that many British officers are expected to be on the train. My brother and his friends are sure they will successfully gain the money for arms. You will be fine."

"We'll see about that."

"Nothing an undercover agent cannot handle, if that is who you say you are." She looked up from her hands and into his eyes. "What about you? How did you get started in the…"

"The Bureau?" He twisted his mouth into a wistful expression. "Doesn't matter."

"Spies?"

Warren picked up the stick she had set down. He began stoking the fire, avoiding her gaze. "We prefer 'information collectors.' Wasn't born in America, but it's the land I've been serving. I came out of university in the States and planned to be a lawyer but quit my first job after it all became too repetitive. A buddy offered me cash to help him with a project."

"What project?"

"I had to go undercover and collect Bertillon records. Heard of those?"

She tilted her head to the side. "I believe so."

"Measurements of the head, body, all sorts of information for criminal identification." He opened his mouth to say something else, then promptly closed it.

"Why did you come out of university in America? You said you were not born there." Words tumbled from her lips in an effort to break down the walls that shut her out. "Where were you born?"

"In India, actually."

Parineeta frowned. "Then how did you end up back ..."

"It's a long story."

She folded her arms over her chest. "I have time, Mr. Warren." Her eyes widened. Warren what? "I do not even know your true identity."

"It's not important right now." He stood and pulled his shirt back on, stretching his arm into the starched sleeves. Parineeta had expected him to continue, but instead he remained silent while he pushed each button carefully through the holes, clearly ignoring her.

She thought about protesting, but a rustling in the bushes made her think twice about making any sound. Holding her breath, she put out the fire with as little noise as possible.

Warren leaned against the thick tree trunk that hid them from one angle and craned his neck. Jungle leaves surrounded them on all sides, but suddenly the protection felt lacking. Parineeta backed up against a nearby tree trunk and watched his hand fall to his pocket, where she knew one of the pistols still lay. She began to hear sounds from the other side of the trunk. Maybe it was just an animal.

But as the noises continued, they grew in clarity until it sounded like chatter. Voices. Clearly British voices. Now she could hear the stomping of heavy boots. She knew British soldiers sometimes patrolled villages in the early morning but never dense jungles in the middle of the night.

"Heard there's a general on the run. Don't know why though," one of the men said. The closer his boots swung toward the direction of their alcove, the louder Parineeta could hear her own heartbeat roaring within her ears. "Lieutenant colonel said they'd be somewhere in this bloody jungle. Do you know anything about the general?"

"Took his secret Indian darkie wife with him, the tale goes. Load of rubbish, if you ask me." The other man seemed to be stepping in the opposite direction. "No respectable gent would dare marry a half-blood coolie."

"Can't be marriage."

The other man snickered. "You're right. Probably just wanted a little fun."

She clenched her fists. It took everything within her to remain silent at the derogatory terms. As if her race did not possess any feeling! As if she were any less of a human than the rest of them!

The men continued to march in silence, and after a few minutes even the sounds of their footsteps faded away. Parineeta couldn't imagine that she would have felt much worse had they actually discovered them.

Warren breathed an audible sigh of relief. "That was close. We need to get out of here." He finished buttoning the top of his shirt. "We'll try to find the nearest town and stay there for…" His voice trailed off. "Are you all right?"

She remained silent, mulling over the men's words. *No one would dare marry a half-blood coolie. No one.*

"I said, are you all right?" He placed a heavy hand on the top of her shoulder. "Is it because of what those men said?"

Perhaps. She remained silent.

"They are wrong, you know. I've never approved of that word."

It was strange how a simple phrase could cause a greater ache than a physical wound. "It wasn't the word; it was the way they used it."

"That no one would ever marry you?" He spoke aloud the words echoing in her mind. "What are you talking about? You're beautiful. You're smarter than any woman I've ever met. Why wouldn't someone marry you?"

The surge of hope and surprise at his compliment was quickly smothered by the reality she recognized within the reply. He was only saying such things to comfort her. "A smart mouth has little value in my village. I am a half-caste, Warren. I do not belong with white men, but no Indian man will ever have me either. All my other friends are married. No respectable family wants to marry a daughter of dirty blood."

"Dirty blood? That's ridiculous." His kindness toward her was a special form of torture. The more he gave, the more Parineeta realized she could never have, not for long, in any case.

"Everyone does." She clenched her fists so the tears would not fall again. She could not count all the times she'd wished her mother had married an Indian man instead of falling for a British soldier. She wished her mother had guarded her heart away, far from the man who wanted nothing to do with her after she fell pregnant. At least her daughter would have had an identity then, instead of an absent father. "The more the tension between the British and Hindustanis grows, the more I am ignored in my village. Raj is my only real friend anymore, and he talks to me because I'm his sister."

"Am I not your friend?" Warren lifted her chin with his thumb and forefinger. Strands of dark hair fell across his forehead, and he swiped it back with his other hand. "I think trusting our lives with one another qualifies us enough to be friends."

Parineeta smiled in spite of herself. She supposed they were. "Yes, we are friends."

"Good." He let go of her chin but remained close. "Do not allow anyone's opinion to cause you to doubt your own worth. Your race determines nothing about who you are."

She nodded. "Of course. It's just difficult when you know there is something about you that you can never change. And everyone seems to think it's all you are. It defines your entire identity."

"It doesn't define a thing. I've only known you for a few days, but I can already tell you are…you are…"

For a single moment, she saw a flicker of desire in his gaze. He leaned forward, his head inclined in her direction. Her heart lurched. She stood still, waiting for his next move.

Then as quickly as she'd seen the look, the longing vanished. He turned his head away from her. Warm air filled the growing space between them, and she felt her heart plummet. Warren cleared his throat as he dusted off the length of his shirt. "We had better get going. There could be other soldiers behind the ones we just heard."

Parineeta stepped back, stunned. Had she only imagined that moment?

Harsh voices cut through the night. "There they are! That has to be them!"

Warren grabbed her hand and started running forward. "And we better get going *now!*"

Her feet sprang into action. They sprinted through the foliage, gripping onto one another's hand. The footsteps behind them grew louder, and so did the voices. She brushed the low-hanging *haldu* leaves in her way as she ran, jumping over each gnarled root of the gigantic tree as her body hurtled through the air. She didn't dare to turn around, fearful of the consequences from slowing down.

"Get them!" a clear, loud voice called out again.

Chapter Six

"Duck!" Warren hissed. She followed his lead and moved her head beneath a low, thick branch before leaping to the other side of the tree. She heard several thumps against the branch behind her as well as low curses. No doubt the men had not followed the same advice Warren had offered her.

The dense vegetation of the teak and *haldu* trees soon gave way to a smooth dirt clearing before a village. No one else wandered the outskirts of the village at this time, with the exception of a motor scooter crossing the road every now and then. Even if the two British soldiers were on a special patrol for her and Warren, at least there didn't seem to be any other soldiers here to back them up. The heavy footsteps and the cries of continued marching could still be heard behind them. Several of the houses before them were lit by lanterns propped up in each of the windowsills.

Parineeta's eyes widened in recognition. "I know this place!" She pointed to a house in the distance, nestled at the end of the road. The town of Bhargain marked a halfway point between her village of Hathras and the train station of Shahjahanpur, but she hadn't anticipated stumbling into it. "My aunt lives there."

"Then that's where we're headed for the night." He ran over to a motorcycle riding by and waved his arms in front of the rider. The vehicle slowed to a bumpy halt. As soon as it stopped, Warren pushed the man off the bike and climbed onto the seat. He motioned for her to sit behind him. "Get on!"

"Sorry!" she called to the rider as she stepped onto the bike behind Warren. Her arms wrapped around his broad chest, and her hands clasped together as she held on tightly.

Once the bike started speeding forward, Parineeta dared to look behind her. The soldiers finally emerged from the forest. She grinned in triumph when they caught her gaze. *You cannot catch us now!*

Her smile faded as soon as she saw them knocking off other motorcycle riders on the same road. Curse their luck! It was uncommon enough for *one* motorcycle to be on the road at such a time at night, much less three! Before the drivers could get back on their bikes, two of the soldiers jumped onto the cycles and sped after Warren. They met her gaze this time with smiles of their own.

She whipped her head back around, pulling her loose tendrils behind her shoulder as the wind whipped at her curls. "Warren! They're still following us!"

He looked down at his mirrors and then back up at the road. She gulped as he revved the engine faster. "Hold on, *pagal ladki.*"

Parineeta wanted to reprimand him for his terrible nickname again, but their motorcycle zoomed down the road with a sudden ferocity that clamped her mouth shut. The roar of new engines edged nearer.

Two motorcycles emerged from both sides of her line of vision as the soldiers tried to approach them. She checked the distance between them out of the corner of her eye, watching with alarm as the barrier of space seemed to close. The night air blew against the folds of her sari. She pressed her arms tighter around Warren until her chest lay flat against his back.

He zipped through the wide entrance of the town and through the narrow alley streets. The soldiers surely could not follow them from both sides as soon as the road tapered. Yet they chased after them through the backstreets, one motorcycle after the other.

Warren skidded against one side of the alley, knocking over a wooden table holding brass pots and tin pans that went clattering to the ground and leaving a trail of metal in their wake. Her own form fell back around the turn and then lurched forward against his body as he settled back into a straight path.

The mess made one of the motorcyclists brake suddenly, which flipped over his bike. The soldier went flying into the air, landing a safe distance from Parineeta and Warren. She watched as the other bike crashed into the one laid on the ground, causing its rider to hurtle off his seat like the first.

She turned back around. "They're gone."

The motorcycle screeched to a halt. Parineeta gritted her teeth and struggled to hold on as gravity attempted to pull her off the bike. She leaned her whole body to the left as the bike swerved to a sharp right.

Once the vehicle slowed to a complete stop, Warren inclined his head toward her. "It's been a while since I could ride like that."

She tucked a lock of hair behind her ear and smoothed out the loose *pallu* of her sari. With the threat of capture removed, she rolled her eyes at Warren. "How they teach you that and not how to build a proper fire, I will never understand. Americans."

One leg over the other and she was off the bike and back on the ground. Warren stepped off the motorcycle after her and then laid the vehicle by a nearby alley wall. The only sounds that could be heard among the alleys were the crunch of their own footsteps against the dirt.

She readjusted the pallu of her sari, shifting the cloth to further cover her bare midriff. "How fast were you planning to go? Kill us by crashing into a wall before the soldiers get to us first?"

"We're here, aren't we?" Even as he spoke, she could hear the uncertainty in his tone.

"Ha! And what do you propose will happen to us when the soldiers report back to the lieutenant colonel?" Did this man never think of consequences?

"So says the revolutionary. And what do you have planned?" He flattened out the edges of his collared shirt.

"Explain to Aunt Ankita that I need a place to stay for the night." Parineeta peered around the corner. The houses were starting to look more familiar. She hadn't been back to the town in years, but her aunt had always welcomed her whenever she'd visited.

A tap on her shoulder brought her attention back to Warren. "You mean *we* need a place to stay for the night. I will speak with your aunt."

"You?" She arched an eyebrow at him. He stood there in the remnants of his uniform regalia: beige pants ripped at the bottom of his thighs, a once-white shirt covered in splotches of dust, a leather belt with a brass buckle as wide as his neck, and long black boots that were faded brown at the toes and extended up to his knees. If her aunt didn't think he had been robbed, she would assume he was a mad beggar. "Not in this state, you aren't."

• • •

He was definitely imagining things. He had to be. There was absolutely no way on earth the man he saw before him was…well, him.

Parineeta had swept his unruly dark hair into a turban, placed him in a tan kameez shirt and added some white shalvar pants.

If she hadn't insisted on dressing him in traditional garb, he would have stayed in his button-up and khaki pants. But the disguising effect had worked. The past few days of walking under the hot sun's rays had tanned his skin darker than it had ever been back in Hathras. He stared at himself through alternating sides of the mirror, examining his reflection from different angles.

"No one will recognize you as a British general now," she said from behind him. She'd read his mind. "Or an American spy."

"What did you say?" The voice of an older woman speaking in Hindi drifted through the fabric curtain.

"Nothing!" Parineeta replied. "Don't worry, aunt."

He raised an eyebrow at her through the mirror. "And does your brother know we're coming with his men?"

She brushed off the top of his seamless kameez. "No, Raj does not." She didn't meet his gaze in the mirror. Her eyes remained fixed on the cloth instead; she was clearly admiring her handiwork. "I know where he will be hiding, though. And I sincerely doubt he will turn away his sister and the man who saved his life."

The sizzle of the frying pan from the kitchen caught Warren's attention. His stomach growled as the scent of fresh eggs and fried naan and creamy butter chicken filled the air.

Parineeta smiled at the sound. "Come, eat with us."

He didn't need to be commanded twice.

His guide led the way, and he followed, brushing aside the thin cloth sheet that acted as a door between the main room and the kitchen. The lack of ventilation in the kitchen caused the hot air from cooking to remain trapped in the room. Tiny wooden stools were perched against the table, and the bowls ranged from battered tin to chipped marbled clay. No silverware lay spread on the table, yet the sight before him seemed grander than any five-course feast he'd ever attended in the queen's honor.

Warren sat down and began eating. His stomach yearned for more food after each bite. He reached for the fried naan, swirled it around in the butter chicken, and polished off all the pieces of paneer in his bowl.

"Your husband is quite hungry!" Parineeta's Aunt Ankita exclaimed.

She gasped. "Oh, he's not my…"

"Thank you. This woman does not feed me enough at home." He felt a swift kick to his left shin beneath the table. He tried to stifle a smirk. "I appreciate you allowing us to stay in your home for the night."

"No inconvenience at all." Ankita set another tin bowl on the table for Parineeta. "I wish this girl would visit me more. It's been so long since I've seen you and Raj." She threw her arms into the air, exasperated with her niece. "You've even married a nice man and haven't told me!"

"He is not your son-in-law." She corrected her aunt with an insistent tone but not before she shot a warning look at Warren.

Her aunt's jaw dropped. "You mean without marriage…you two already…"

"She jokes, of course." He nearly laughed aloud when he saw Parineeta flush with embarrassment. She looked mortified. He picked up another piece of naan and bit off a section of the delicious flatbread. "We are married, aren't we, *pagal ladki?*"

Ankita giggled, shoving Warren's shoulder in a playful way. "You shouldn't call your wife such names."

His "wife" crossed the floor to the other side of the room. She lifted the cloth separating the two rooms and left the kitchen without another word.

"Oh!" Ankita frowned. "Was it something I said?"

He pursed his lips and set his bread back down in his bowl. If he'd learned anything from living among the British gentry, it was that it was always best to apologize first.

He found her leaning against one of the walls and staring out the window at the dusty, narrow street.

"Parineeta, I'm sorry." Warren stepped forward, his brown sandals slapping against the dirt floor. He placed a hand on her arm, and her shoulders stiffened underneath his touch. "I shouldn't have joked about your marriage."

"Why wouldn't you?" Her voice stretched tight, firm and defiant. All traces of warmth had left her tone. "You, the white male, can have any woman you want."

The white male? He frowned. "What are you talking about?"

He was sure that if he could take one look at her face, he'd see the return of her familiar fiery gaze. "You can have any white woman and any Indian woman, just as you please. You don't care at all about their feelings, so long as your own needs are met."

He furrowed his brow. "I am not like that, Parineeta."

She whirled around. "Yes, you are. You're all the same. My father abandoned my mother, just like you would abandon any woman…"

"Parineeta!" He grabbed both of her shoulders. She stood there, silent before him. That proud chin of hers tilted upward. The last time she'd given him such a fierce gaze was right before they'd entered the ballroom back at his mansion. "Not all men are the same. Not all men will betray you."

"Yes? Then what do you plan to do once you reach Lucknow?"

Warren dropped his hands. His chest ached at the thought of keeping more information from her. He couldn't reveal everything…not yet. There was too much to explain. *Raj.* He couldn't forget to keep tabs on her brother, nor could he afford to let Parineeta know.

"It doesn't matter." Her gaze had fallen from his face and was fixed on something behind him.

She probably thought the worst of him. Humidity surrounded them all on sides, trapping his untold secrets in the heat. If he did have reason to suspect her brother of anarchist influence, he would have no choice but to inform his bureau chief. Would she even speak to him if she discovered his true reason for spying?

"Warren." Her voice sounded clipped, and her wide eyes filled with panic. "Go to the kitchen. Don't turn around, and get back into the other room right now."

"Why?" He stepped forward, but her outstretched hand pushed him back.

"Soldiers. Outside." She inclined her head toward the kitchen, all the while keeping her eyes trained on the scene outside the window. "Now *go.*"

Of course the lieutenant colonel would send more soldiers to the village where they had last been seen. He swallowed hard and marched toward the kitchen. They should've left earlier in the morning. Damn him for getting too comfortable in one place. Within seconds, she was inside the room as well.

Parineeta's aunt was in the process of pouring water over some of the dishes. She moved with a slow pace, oblivious to the soldiers outside her home.

He watched the woman beside him march toward her aunt and place a gentle hand on her arm. "Aunty, we have to leave."

Ankita sighed and set aside one of the tin bowls. "You just arrived."

Warren placed his back flat against one wall and twisted his shoulders to peer through the glass window. Five British soldiers marched down the street in a pack of pith helmets and pressed brown uniforms, asking questions of Indian men passing by. The Indians they talked to were well-dressed in newsboy caps and collared shirts with gray pants fit for a proper suit. There was little fear in their postures, unlike the poorer villagers he had seen before. Maybe it had nothing to do with their level of wealth. Perhaps the revolutionary fever merely coated this village thicker than the others.

Each Indian in the group shrugged his shoulders and shook his head, but the soldiers still seemed to be walking in his and Parineeta's direction all the same.

His attention flickered from the soldiers to the scene inside the kitchen once Parineeta spoke again. "It's urgent. I will be in contact with you soon. Don't worry."

He turned around and jerked a thumb over his shoulder. "There's no time to lose."

Ankita grabbed one of his hands and surrounded his palm with both of hers. Wrinkles pulled up against the sides of her mouth as she smiled at him. Her touch was warm. "I hope your journey to Lucknow will be safe."

"I hope so, too. I cannot thank you enough for your kindness and hospitality," he said in Hindi. He placed his other palm over the top of the woman's weathered hands.

She leaned in closer. Her green veil fell forward on her forehead until it covered her gray hair. "Take good care of my Parineeta, won't you?"

He didn't need to think twice. "I will protect her with my life."

An unceremonious snort echoed from the other room. When had Parineeta left the kitchen?

"He needs my protection as well!"

"That I do!" The corner of his mouth quirked upward as he left the room to join her.

Crazy girl.

• • •

Parineeta pushed aside one of the low swinging branches of the mango tree. The sticky air around her smelled damp, cool, and fresh. Even after she'd disguised Warren, she felt much more comfortable traveling through the dense jungle than through populous towns and villages. The last problem they needed was someone recognizing either of them on the main road.

"Look what I found!"

She turned around at the sound of his excited voice. He stood a few feet away from her, pointing to a mango tree. A plethora of ripe, juicy mangoes drooped down from the branches, just above his head.

She frowned. "All you think about is your stomach." She searched the branches above the mangoes for any other signs of life up there. "There will be food when we find my brother. Let us continue on for now."

But Warren jumped up anyway, grabbing a mango and yanking the fruit off the tree. He grabbed another and another. She walked over to him and placed both of her hands on his shoulders.

"Stop!"

He halted with a jerky motion. The confusion etched across his brow almost made her laugh. His hands clenched around the reddish-orange fruits. "Why should I?"

As if on cue, she heard the familiar sound of the tree's inhabitants and felt dread sink into the pit of her stomach. She swiped at the fruits to try to knock them out of his hands, but he extended his arm up and away to keep the mangoes just out of her reach. "Because those do not belong to you."

"That's ridiculous." Warren held up his fruit to the light, admiring his prize as if it had been given to him from Vishnu himself. "Who else could they belong to?"

A series of screeches from above answered his question.

"*Aye Bhagwan*," she murmured.

Nearly a dozen monkeys began to descend the length of the mango tree's branches to stare at Warren. Each set of beady, hazel eyes poked out of fuzzy, pink faces framed with thin coats of brown fur. Their ears pricked up, aware of the intruder. She could have sworn they were scowling. Silence filled the air for several moments.

She remained still, while he backed up against her. Yet the monkeys continued to climb down the branches, gathering in size until even she felt her jaw drop.

Before she could say a word, the group started emitting a loud, high-pitched bark. The largest monkey bared its teeth at Warren with a hiss.

He dropped the mangoes, sending all the fruit he'd gathered rolling across the floor.

She sucked in a quick intake of breath. "On the count of three, you are following me…"

"You have a plan?"

"No."

"Oh."

"One…"

Suddenly, one of the monkeys in the back flew into the air, its arms outstretched as it missed Warren by a few centimeters. He swore. The monkey screeched again, and the others followed his example.

"Three! Go!" She took off, heading deeper into the jungle. His heavy footsteps thudded behind her, accompanying the sounds of his continual cursing in streams of English phrases she'd never heard before.

The monkeys were never far behind them, screaming shrill threats. She saw them out of the corner of her eye swing from tree to tree to keep up.

"This way!" Parineeta ducked beneath another branch as her feet hurried along the edge of a wide boulder until the rock merged with a dark cave. She ran inside the narrow opening, with Warren following just seconds behind her. The farther they ran, the more the sound of monkeys died out.

He hung his head, wheezing for breath as he put his hands on his knees. The once pristine kameez pants were covered in dirt around the ankles. "I knew I would be outrunning the British on this mission, but I never thought about the monkeys."

"You stole their food." She frowned. "They had every right to be angry at you."

He held up his hands. There were scratches on his palms and along his forearms, probably where he'd brushed against a branch. "All right, I will never attempt to steal from nature again. You saved my life back there."

She nodded. "Good. It might not be the last time. If you respect the jungle, then the jungle will respect you."

"And what about people?"

"People do not respect you even if you respect them."

He remained quiet for a moment. The cave blocked out sounds from outside and let little light waft in through the opening. Still, she could make out his soft expression. "I know what you mean."

The corner of her mouth twisted into a wry smile. Of course he did not. Still, it was sweet of him to empathize. She raised her veil from around her shoulders to cover the sides of her head.

"How do you know so much about the jungle, anyway?" He leaned against one side of the cave, and she watched his face slip into the shadows. "I thought your entire family worked for the previous general who lived in that house before me. Surely he didn't send you out for tasks in the trees."

The unbidden memories sent a fresh wave of pain straight to her heart. "When I was younger, I worked as a maid in the house. But the previous general was… He would instruct me to scrub the floors from dawn until sundown, when I would finally receive a break to eat a meal. All his servants were treated in such a manner."

"Why?"

"I do not believe he saw us as people. We were simply 'coolies' who could be worked like dogs. I would often escape into the jungle, and eventually I no longer worked in the house at all."

"I see." Warren reached out to envelope both of her hands into his smooth ones. She flinched. Yet as her skin grew accustomed to the touch, she relaxed her hands in his. It alarmed her how much more at ease she was becoming around him. It was almost as if he provided a source of comfort, something she couldn't quite name and didn't care to. "I do not understand why anyone would be cruel to you, though."

He rubbed his thumb in a circular motion over her hand. Shockwaves from his touch jolted up her arm.

Danger. She wrenched one of her hands from his hold and pivoted on her heel. But his right hand still gripped hers with firm pressure. Her torso twisted as she kept her face turned from his. "Then you do not know enough of the world."

"I think I do." His voice was low and husky. A chill ran up Parineeta's spine and unfamiliar heat pooled in the pit of her stomach. "I've seen and known many women during my life. No agent's or colonel's daughter has ever been more courageous or intelligent than you."

Parineeta spun her head around. She wanted—no, she needed—to believe this man. No one had ever said the honeyed words that left his mouth to her before. They were so sweet that she could almost taste her grandmother's syrup. He squeezed her hand and brought her body ever so closer to his. His musky scent lingered in the air, and she would have sworn he could hear her heartbeat.

"You called me intelligent in the past. Am I?" She lifted her chin, reclaiming her pride and throwing off whatever feeling this man gave her. She would not buckle to her knees before him. "I am here to learn information from you and nothing more, yet you seem to draw me into dangerous situations."

Warren lifted his thumb to graze the top of her cheekbone. She struggled to keep her breathing under control as she met his gaze. The brown hair she had grown accustomed to seeing so coiffed and slicked back had fallen from its former grace and hung loose over his forehead, the ends brushing the top of his eyes.

When he spoke, he sounded distant, as if in a trance. His eyes remained fixed on hers. "I wish every woman was like you."

She felt her cheeks flush. No man had ever spoken to her with such boldness before. A heady rush swept through her body as he inched closer to her, removing the gap between them as he inclined his body toward hers. His stubble scratched the side of her cheek, and his scent bombarded her senses, removing all rational thought. It was only her and him, in this moment, free and alive and closer and closer....

His lips brushed against hers, softly at first, then more insistent. She clutched the collar of his kameez. Could he hear her heart pounding? His right hand threaded through her hair, combing through her waves and falling along the sides of her sari. His other hand pressed into the small of her back, molding her body against his.

Her body naturally reacted in the same way—hungry and yearning against his lips. She put everything she had into the kiss, all her years of rejection and feeling unwanted and being unable to marry due to her skin. Too dark for the British to view her as an equal, too light for the men in her village to forget who her father was. She'd never kissed a man before. And this one made her feel like a flame burning up from the tips of her toes to the top of her head.

Chapter Seven

He pressed her further back against the cool stone behind her. His body covered hers as she arched against him and wrapped one of her legs around his waist. Warmth filled her to the core. She needed more. Her hands fell to the hardened muscles of his upper arms as her hair fanned out against the cave wall behind her.

The weight of his body felt amazing against her own. He pushed further against her, running his hand up and down her arm as his chest covered hers. She'd never known such heat before. Her hands fell from his arms to roam down the length of his back, where her palms splayed against his chiseled muscles. She moaned against his neck when he drew away for breath, unable to trap the sound inside her.

He paused and rested his forehead against her own. When he spoke, he drew in ragged breaths between each word. "Parineeta, I think I may…"

A cold hand gripped her heart. "Stop."

He looked up, confusion furrowing his brow. "What?"

She glanced down at their position. One of her legs wrapped tightly against his waist, while the other had drifted up the back of his ankle. What was she doing? How could she? She pushed him off her, sending him reeling backward. "Stop. Do not say one more word."

He tried to reach for her arm, but she held up one hand in warning.

"I am not my mother," she whispered.

His face fell.

"My mother fell for a man's words once, too. He had no interest in her soul, only an interest in her body. She believed he loved her." Parineeta swallowed hard. "I will not make her mistake."

He let out a deep exhale. "Why are you comparing me to him?"

"Why wouldn't I? You are all the same."

"I would never abandon you."

"I hardly know you!"

He stepped back at her exclamation. The force of her words startled even her. "I am supposed to use you as a tool for revenge, not a man to fall in love with. I have no time to..." To what? To care for someone? Surely not to fall in love.

"Neither did I. I always thought I needed to leave for my next assignment, that there was no point in settling down with any girl." Warren set his jaw. His shoulders stiffened. "Parineeta, I didn't plan this."

She hated the way her name sounded on his lips, so tender and so tinged with desire, hated it more than the torrential monsoon rains, more than the endless days when the past general had worked her to the bone. At least they didn't offer her a glimpse of something she'd never have. "I will not fall for your sweet words and flattery. I know better than to trust men like you." She looked away.

Warren stepped toward her, a few twigs crackling beneath his weight. She remained fixed to the spot, avoiding his gaze. The closer he came, the more her body ached with longing. Her chest rose and fell with each purposeful breath she took, determined to calm herself.

His breath was hot against her cheek. "How can I prove it to you?"

"You can't."

Without another word, Parineeta stormed out of the cave.

• • •

Warren banged his fist against the cave wall. Pain flooded his arm, but that didn't stop him from punching the rock's surface one more time. How could he have been so *stupid!*

What in the world had possessed him to kiss her so suddenly? No wonder she'd thought he'd tried to take advantage of her. What had he been thinking? He rested one hand against the stone wall, biting his curled forefinger as he brought his fist to his mouth. He hadn't been thinking, of course. His body had gravitated toward her, guided by nothing other than the incredible softness of her skin and the instinctual need for sensation. He hadn't even realized what was happening until she'd pushed him away.

He shut his eyes, trying to will the image of the half-Indian beauty from his mind. How her lithe body had felt beneath him, how he'd been pressed so close against her full hips… He clenched his fists. Now she'd never let him touch her again.

He'd thought she was pretty when he first met her, but somehow she drew him in further each time he saw her. She was beautiful in an effortless, unassuming way. It was as if the sharpness of her features and the sensuality of her frame had magnified until he could no longer ignore them. She really had no idea about her effect on him.

One moment he'd simply been grateful that she'd saved his life, and the next moment he'd found himself clinging to her kisses, unable to let go. There was something different about her. Something daring, even adventurous. Maybe it was the fact that she was a spy, too.

He wanted to laugh. What was that phrase the NBCI instructors repeated to all new recruits during training? *Don't fall in love.* He'd never had a problem with the simple mandate until that moment, when he was running from the damn British army and had to go to Lucknow to deliver confidential information for the American government.

He frowned. She'd been right to push him away. He couldn't give her what she deserved. Stability and social acceptance would always elude her as long as she was with him. Neither of those two ways of life had ever been his, and he had no desire to claim them for his own. He could only give her a life on the run. *She deserves far better.*

Warren walked outside to join her…and stopped dead in his tracks. Waiting for him stood several men with their fists curled around guns, tapping the weapons against their free hands. The expressions on all their faces were severe as they studied him, trying to make out who he was.

"Ah, there he is!"

He turned his head at the sound of Raj's voice. Parineeta stood next to her brother. Her own expression was blank, and her lips were pressed together into a tight line.

Raj was holding a gun in each hand, the revolvers down at his sides. He smiled. "My sister tells me you have decided to join us. The more of us at work, the more successful the mission will be. You may accompany us to Lucknow."

Parineeta finally looked up at Warren. Her blank expression was replaced by one of amusement. "I believe you know my brother. These are his friends. They belong to the freedom fighter group called the Hindustan Republican Association."

She gestured to the men surrounding them on all sides. The band of anarchists, or so the NBCI had feared they were, looked like any other men—collared shirts, grey vests, pressed pants. None of them could have been over the age of thirty.

One man with a thin mustache stepped forward. He seemed the strongest of the group. His arms were crossed in front of him, but he nodded to Warren. "Ashfaqulla Khan."

Another man, this one without any guns, also stepped forward. He was slightly rounder than Ashfaqulla, a white fedora perched on his head. "Bismil."

The other men introduced themselves in turn, each regarding Warren with a wary eye. Nevertheless, he felt a sense of acceptance within their circle. It seemed that Raj's friendly salute was enough to convince them to trust a stranger for the time being. There were seven people in total, and, according to Parineeta, more would join them at the station.

They set up camp for the night. Warren continually tried to speak with Parineeta, but she ignored him each time he approached her. The moment he entered within a few yards of her, she would immediately start talking to one of Raj's friends. The routine repeated itself until he finally gave up. It was time to focus his attentions instead to helping the other men find firewood.

He set to work picking up pieces of wood outside the official camp. The men who had introduced themselves as Ashfaqulla and Bismil were not far away.

Ashfaqulla strapped his lanky arm around Warren's shoulder. "How does a white man like you end up fighting an Indian's battle?"

He stiffened, but Ashfaqulla patted his back in a reassuring manner. "I mean you no harm. Do not worry; your secret is safe. Raj told us who you are."

"It is Parineeta, is it not?" Bismil pointed in the direction of the camp behind Warren. "She is your reason for joining us."

"I have several reasons," Warren responded in unaccented Hindi. Even if they knew he was a foreigner, there was no reason to act like one. "She was never one of them before."

"Ah, but she is a reason now! It is only a matter of time before two people who embark on a journey together share their souls. Your situation is fit for poetry." Ashfaqulla grinned. He held up his other hand in the air and swept it in her direction. "She likes you too, it seems. She keeps looking over here."

Warren glanced back at the camp. Parineeta stood next to some of the other men, but her gaze was focused on him. Her eyes widened when they locked with his, as if caught in a criminal act. She inclined her head away, and he could already see the beginning of a bright flush bloom at the tops of her cheeks.

Unbidden hope surged within his chest.

After the fire was built, the men unpacked what little food they had and shared it among themselves. The smells of biryani, potatoes, and spices filled the air. Discussion of paneer swung into debates of politics as the food dwindled down and the embers of the fire continued to flicker.

"Non-violence should be the first method we attempt," Parineeta instructed the group of men. All of the revolutionaries listened in silence. Ashfaqulla had finished his prayers for the day and joined the circle around Parineeta to hear her as well. While the other men said nothing to contradict her, they shifted around the fire and threw glances at one other, their faces displaying unease.

Caste and race and religion didn't matter in this independence movement. The garb of the men around the fire all suggested different economic backgrounds. The desire to be free surpassed all other differences.

"But how can we continue to be non-violent, sister, when they attack us with clubs?" Raj spun the gun in his hand, watching the flames dance across the shining barrel of his revolver. "We've waited long enough. These soft expressions of non-violence may win us sympathy, but it will not win us independence."

"He is right!" Bismil tapped his fist against his other palm. He stood up as he continued. "We must use guns for this robbery!"

Parineeta held up one hand in a halting motion but kept her voice even. "We may use them to threaten the soldiers but not to kill anyone. Fighting fire with fire will only result in the whole world in flames. We do not want to cause suffering in India, only peace within our borders."

"Bullets will achieve peace," Raj deadpanned. He looked up from his gun and inclined his head in Warren's direction. "What do you think of using violence for tomorrow's robbery?"

"Violence may lead to anarchy. If your mission is to remove the concept of a state entirely, then violence will serve." Warren studied Raj's expression.

To his surprise, the young revolutionary widened his eyes at Warren's statement. "Is that what you think of us? Anarchists?" He chewed the last of his meal for several seconds, as if mulling over the words. "We want a government of self-rule. We wish to unite India under one government, not destroy India's unification."

Warren had found no concrete evidence of Raj Singh's anarchist influence, and here he was, declaring that he had no interest in anarchy! Perhaps the NBCI had the wrong information. Still, it was better to wait it out and see what else Raj admitted about his independence movement.

"No one should be harmed. The guns should be used simply as a threat." Warren glanced at Parineeta. "She has a point. Violence will only cause more of the British to be angry at you without understanding your cause."

"Hear, hear!" Ashfaqulla clapped. "I approve of what this man says. Violence as necessary but not as the first option." He nudged Parineeta, who sat next to him. "You have found a man with wise advice."

Her forehead creased at his words. She cut a quick glare at Warren as if he'd said something explicitly inappropriate. Before he could apologize for something he hadn't said, she excused herself from the circle.

He stood and followed her. A few cries and teases came from the other men, but he ignored them.

The moonlight shined through the tops of the trees, and the leaves cast scattered shadows along the forest floor. Parineeta stood in a clearing a few yards away from the main part of the camp, her arms folded across her chest.

He cleared his throat.

"Why did you follow me?"

"I came to see if you were all right."

"I am." She lifted her chin. "Now go."

He smirked. *Always so proud.* He decided to press his luck and stepped closer to Parineeta. "They listen to you. All of the men do."

She tapped her foot and drew her sari tighter around her. "What are you talking about?"

"They respect you."

"That doesn't mean they will…" She shook her head. "Forget it."

The words left unsaid hung in the air. She'd said none of the other men from her village wished to marry her, but surely she could see that they admired her intelligence. Could she see how he admired her? "I respect you."

The foot tapping stopped, and her shoulders drooped. "What do you respect about me?"

"That you are independent. You're fiery. You aren't afraid to voice your opinions, and that's what causes people to listen to you. You're not afraid of anything." Warren suddenly realized that he could continue on and on about all the reasons. It was a new feeling, this ability to speak so much about someone. He moved toward her, half-expecting her to walk away.

She stood rooted to the spot instead. He couldn't see her face, but her voice trembled. "I am not used to anyone being so forward."

"Maybe no one ever expressed himself before."

She looked up toward the sky. "You are wrong."

Warren closed the distance between them. He could hear her breathing, heavy and uneven. "About what?"

"Not being afraid." She turned around. The pale moonlight splashed across her face, the gentle, white light highlighting her cheekbones. "I am afraid."

"Of what?"

"Of you."

He kissed her full lips again, lightly at first. The moonlight shined between the treetops above them, forming a spotlight on where they stood. He felt her fingers run through his hair, weaving down the sides and toward the nape of his neck.

She keened against his lips, and he felt his lower half tighten at the sound. Still, he resisted the urge to pull her closer. What if she feared him taking advantage of her? He couldn't risk losing her trust so soon.

But she pressed against him anyway, wrapping both of her legs around his waist as he held her up. She turned her head to the side, and her neck lay exposed before him. He leaned downward, laying her body against the grass. Her eyelids were shut, and rays of moonlight bathed over both of them.

She overwhelmed him.

Her wavy hair splayed out against the grass, loose and wild. He wrapped a dark tendril around his finger, curling the lock toward the base.

Parineeta arched against him, and he groaned before he could stop himself. This woman would drive him mad. His lips found the juncture of her neck and shoulder blade, where he peppered insistent kisses. She wrapped both of her arms around his neck and pressed his body closer to hers.

As the pale moonlight washed both of them in serene light, he held Parineeta's soft body in his arms and realized that she wasn't the only one who was afraid. All his life, he'd lived recklessly with nothing holding him back.

But now he had someone to lose. Someone that was more beautiful and clever and indispensable than anyone else he'd ever met. He wasn't just afraid.

He was terrified.

Chapter Eight

Sunlight streamed through the cracks beneath Parineeta's eyelids, distracting her from sleep. She groaned, turning over to the side to edge closer to the warm comfort of Warren…and found cold ground.

Her eyes flickered open. Her sari lay over her, covering her entire body. Its faded green nearly blended in with the color of the grass beneath her. She pulled the veil over her head as she sat up.

Wind rustled through the tree branches, but the cool breeze contrasted the otherwise damp heat that surrounded her. She stood up, inspecting the area. The grass was flattened from where she and Warren had fallen asleep. *Aye Bhagwan*, what had possessed her?

She bit her lip. Scorching heat, entangled limbs, desperate release. Everything had seemed so perfect in that moment. The harsh light of day cast an entirely different illumination on the night before.

She joined the other men loading their guns. Warren spoke to her brother apart from the others in a hushed tone. His eyes locked with hers. Neither said a word. Was she supposed to start the conversation? Did he think her a fool for spending the night with him?

Her brother, on the other hand, seemed overjoyed to see her. "Sister! Where were you last night? Warren said he went to look for you and then returned back to the camp."

"I was…resting underneath a better place in the moonlight." Parineeta shot a silent look of gratitude to Warren. At least her brother didn't know. "I must have fallen asleep and not realized it."

"Well, we're all here now." Bismil made a final count of the men. Seeming satisfied, he picked up his guns from the ground.

"Station's this way." He headed down one of the worn paths twisting through the trees, and the other men followed.

Warren walked ahead with her brother, leaving her to trail the group from the back. She tried to smother the waves of disappointment rolling through her heart. So he no longer wanted to talk to her? He'd abandoned her after all.

How could she be so foolish? To think she'd believed he'd cared about her, when all he'd desired from her was her body. Her fingers trembled at the truth. She had made her mother's mistake.

• • •

They boarded the Number 8 Down train at Shahjahanpur with little ceremony. Dev, one of her brother's closest friends, had planned most of the robbery. All the money was in a safe placed in the railway guard's carriage. Dev had forced the group to commit the facts to memory over the fire the previous night.

They'd even planned who would sit in which area of the train and how many would be in each compartment. Dev, Parineeta, and Warren all sat together in the center of the train.

Dev placed one arm over Parineeta's shoulder as soon as they sat down. He performed a quick scan of the people sitting around them, checking to make sure no stray ears heard their plans. "I want you to be the one to pull the train to an emergency stop."

She glanced at the drooping chain hung above each of the windows, the chain that would set their plan in motion. "I will. Raj already told me."

"Good." He cleared his throat. "There is something else I must ask you."

She tried to shift her shoulder out from under Dev's hold, but he still held his arm in place. Her back stiffened against the wooden seat. Dev had never gripped her with such firmness before.

"This will come as a surprise to you." He brushed his mustache with one hand, then pulled aside one of the curtains to peer out the window. "But I have asked your brother for your hand in marriage."

What? He had to be joking! She checked Dev's face for any hint of humor. She'd always thought he was handsome, but there was nothing about him that attracted her as more than a friend. "Dev..."

Warren stood suddenly and headed toward the door, leading to the space separating the different areas of the train. He didn't glance back at her.

"You don't have to decide right now." Dev shushed her. "I know your blood makes this marriage less than desirable, Parineeta, but I am willing to overlook that."

She clenched her fists into the material of her sari. Her blood was not dirty. "I would never marry a man who defines me by my race."

Dev's tone became firm. His grip on her shoulder tightened. "I have watched you for a while now."

Was that supposed to be a compliment? She stared out the window for several moments, watching the flattened plains roll by. India's independence was her priority, not whether or not a man 'watched' her.

"I was conflicted because of your half-caste status...no one else will marry you."

Through gritted teeth, she managed to respond. "That does not matter."

"You must take my offer."

The British soldier's words echoed in the back of her mind. *No one would dare marry a half-blood coolie.*

"Dev, I will sit here and do your bidding and pull down the emergency stop when you signal for me to do so." She kept her voice low to avoid drawing attention from the other passengers, but she wanted nothing better than to slap him across the face. "But after this, I never want to speak to you again."

Dev scowled. He stood up and walked in the opposite direction of where Warren had gone, no doubt headed to meet Bismil and check on the compartment which held the money.

"You will regret this," he said before he slammed the door shut.

Other passengers seemed alarmed at the outburst, and several gave her pitying looks. She ignored the whispers around her. So much for trying not to draw attention to herself.

Parineeta continued to sit still for a few moments longer. Adrenaline coursed through her veins. She would rather marry no one than marry someone who refused to see beyond her birth. At the moment, the only person who could make sense of the situation was Warren. She needed to hear his vote of confidence in her, even if he didn't say the words. With a sigh, she rose to find him.

She opened the door to the next compartment to see Warren standing just outside. One of his hands gripped the railing while both eyes were fixed on the rolling landscape before them as the train sped by the dry plains.

She was sure the steam from the engine and the plow of the wheels against the railroad would have disguised the sound of her steps. Yet Warren didn't need to turn around before he said, "Have you accepted?"

Parineeta folded her arms over her chest. Was that why he'd left? "No. I did not accept Dev's proposal."

He tensed his shoulders, and she swore she saw his knuckles whiten as he tightened his hold on the smooth railing. He glanced behind one shoulder at her, his blue-green eyes searching. "And why not?"

"He said he would marry me in spite of my heritage." *In spite.* The words nearly made her laugh. She'd thought of her mixed race in spite plenty of times, but Dev's view of race as a barrier between them provided a whole new definition to the phrase. "I do not see my race as a defining factor, so why should he?"

"And do you care for him?"

"I never have."

"What a shame." But nothing in Warren's voice seemed to point to any actual empathy. Parineeta caught the beginning of a smile quirk against the side of his mouth. Their eyes locked again, and the train and the rolling hills and everything else seemed to melt into the background. "So Kakori is where we stop."

"Near the village of Kakori. Once it's done, we'll all escape to Lucknow from there. I am to pull the emergency stop."

He raised an eyebrow. "You're not afraid of what's about to take place?"

"It will help us fund the independence movement. I never fear independence." *Just certain American spies.*

Warren smiled. He lifted up his hand to place a stray lock of hair behind her ear and then dropped his hand, as if the touch scalded his skin. A clouded look of worry entered his eyes.

"What is it?" She couldn't help the impatience from creeping into her tone. He acted as if he was walking across hot coals around her.

He rubbed his jaw. "I don't want your brother to be suspicious."

"What does it matter?" She puffed out her chest. Really, her brother was no excuse for him to ignore her. "I am old enough to decide for myself what man I choose."

"I'm not the type of man for you."

Her heart sank. Maybe she was wrong. Maybe he still planned to abandon her after all. "You can't...you can't just leave." *Not after last night.* Her voice hardened. No, she would not allow him the satisfaction of knowing how the past night had affected her. "Was this your plan all along?"

"No, of course not!" He let out a sound of frustration. "There was no plan. I cannot give you the life you deserve. I cannot give you stability, safety..."

"And the life I've already chosen for myself is full of stability and safety?" She placed a hand on her hip. Did he believe her to be weak-willed? "My life has as much danger as yours, in case you failed to notice. The independence movement will only grow from this day forward, and I plan to be a part of it every step of the way."

He didn't respond, at least not right away. Instead, he pulled her against him and wrapped his arms around her. She closed her eyes as he held her tightly. Her brother and his friends had always written love poems to other girls in their village, but she'd never understood the lines until now.

She felt him smooth her hair with his hand, and he pressed a kiss to her forehead. "You have such fire inside you, Parineeta."

Her throat constricted. "You've brought it out of me, it seems."

He continued to hold onto her, as if he was afraid she would suddenly slip from his grasp. "In all my years of service, that is the highest honor anyone has ever paid me."

As much comfort as she derived from his compliments, a question tugged at her mind. "Are you going to finally tell me why you are headed to Lucknow?"

"Another officer is stationed there. I need to meet him."

Her heart ran cold. So that was why he had seemed distant this morning. He planned to leave her in Lucknow, didn't he? He would join with other spies, they would give him a safe passage to America, and then she would never see or hear from him again. He had known all along that he would leave her.

Still, the thoughts seemed too harsh to be reality. Perhaps she was getting ahead of herself. "And have you fulfilled your mission, whatever it was?"

His embrace loosened. "Parineeta, they want me to return home. That's what I need to talk to them about."

Her voice trembled. "America?"

"They sent me a letter a few weeks ago instructing me to return as soon as possible. They knew my identity was going to be compromised." He kissed the top of Parineeta's forehead again. "Thank you for taking me this far to Lucknow."

She stepped away. All the pieces started fitting together, slowly at first and then gaining speed. All the signs pointed to his ultimate abandonment. Her worst nightmare had somehow materialized. She'd fallen for a man who planned to leave her as soon as he found the nearest city.

"I would have never been able to reach this far had it not been for you. My mission here was to discover... Well, it was to discover whether or not there was anarchist activity among the revolutionaries. Your brother was the one I was supposed to watch."

Her jaw dropped. "But he's not..."

"An anarchist? I know now. I thought I'd have more time to investigate, but my branch has folded into the FBI and god knows where they'll assign me next." Warren ran a hand through his hair, the dark locks she loved so much now seeming dull in the mid-afternoon light. "To be honest, I'd nearly given up on learning anything at all until I spoke to you."

"Was your mission successful?"

He held one hand against the railing, and the other hand held hers. "Thanks to you, it has been. Now I can report back to the officers in Lucknow and tell them that there is no need to worry about anarchist influence spreading from here to America."

His words drenched her like ice water. He'd used her. He'd wanted her information; he'd wanted her connection to her brother. Not her, though. Never her.

She dropped his hand.

"Parineeta?" His voice was filled with worry. Was it even genuine, or deceiving like the rest of his words? "Where are you going?"

She gulped. "I think I need to sit back down."

"All right, I'll join you."

"No." She held up a hand. Tears started welling in the corners of her eyes, but she blinked them back. There was no way she would let him see her cry. It was her own fault for falling in love with a foreigner who had no intentions of staying. "You stay there and wait for their signal. Then tell me when to stop the train."

She ignored his protests and walked back into the corridor, clicking the door shut behind her. She hurried to her seat and faced the window. The backs of her hands wiped away the tears falling down her cheeks in steady streams. He'd never revealed any intention of remaining with her beyond Lucknow. How could she have been so blind?

She tried to focus on the rolling hillside outside, on the sunshine and the sticky air and when the next monsoon rain would occur. She attempted to concentrate on future plans for the independence movement, on other armories to steal weapons from and other locations to rob for much needed funds.

But all her thoughts kept coming back to Warren.

• • •

Warren could see Dev's and Bismil's forms on the top of the train. He watched as they crouched across the roof of the metal compartment, inching along the top of the speeding locomotive. He waited for their sign.

Dev held Bismil's legs as he leaned him over the railway guard's carriage. Bismil's upside-down body dangled over the ground, the velocity of the train swaying him back and forth. Warren held his breath as the man swung in front of the window for several seconds. At any moment, one of the soldiers might glance out the window, and the whole event could be called off. After what seemed like ages, he tapped Dev's arm, and then Dev pulled him back up again.

Now they were discussing something with each other. A worried look crossed Dev's features. That was strange. He expected Dev's hand to raise in the air, giving him the approval to stop the train. But there was no signal.

Finally, Bismil made a slashing movement against his throat and shook his head in Warren's direction. Warren nodded and mimicked the same slashing movement against his own throat to Bismil. So the robbery would not happen. There were probably too many British soldiers on guard in the compartment, protecting the money from the government treasury.

Parineeta's "information" was that there would be few people on the train. His stomach tightened. He could imagine her crestfallen expression when she learned of the failed plan.

He pushed open the compartment door and marched back inside. Parineeta stood when he entered the carriage. Without waiting for him to speak, she yanked the emergency chain to stop the train.

"Stop!" Warren held onto the back of one of the leather seats for a better grip as the train lurched to a sudden halt. What was she doing? "Bismil called it off."

She reached into the inside of her sari, drew out a gun, and tossed it to him. He barely caught it in time, and then she pulled out another revolver from her sari. "We're not listening to him. It's too late to stop now!"

She marched down the aisles with her gun in the air. Passengers screamed. He walked behind her, lifting his gun up as well.

"Do not be afraid! No Hindustani will be hurt!" Her cries did little to ease the startled passengers. She jumped out at the end of the compartment, and he followed after her. They tapped the carriage sides with their guns, the barrels rattling against the brown metal of the train compartments.

"Close your windows!" Warren yelled. "No one will be harmed. Close your windows!"

Bismil and Dev nearly ran into Parineeta from the other side. Bullets were already whizzing over their heads from where they'd stood on top of the compartment.

"Are you mad?" Dev seethed. He grabbed her, and both of them ducked when a fresh round of gunfire echoed from incoming British soldiers.

Warren wrenched Parineeta away. "Get your hands off of her!"

Raj jumped out from the compartment nearest to them. "Stop bickering! Lal and I will collect the cash. You keep off the soldiers."

A bullet whizzed past Parineeta from Raj's position, making direct contact with the stomach of a British soldier who'd snuck up behind her wielding a club. The guard groaned and dropped to the floor.

Raj and one of his friends headed to the guard's cabin where the money bags from the British treasury were supposed to be. Dev scowled at Warren, but he backed away. All of them ducked at the fire from the guns coming from the other compartment.

Bullets zinged past Warren's head and sank into the metal of the train compartments. He turned his body to shield Parineeta. But she was gone. She'd dashed to the other side, tapping her gun against the sides of the train and yelling for more passengers to close their windows.

"Dev! Behind you!" Warren knocked out the advancing British soldier, and Dev quickly shot him. Another bullet whizzed by his shoulder blade, causing the hairs on the back of his neck to bristle.

Warren pulled out his gun and took careful aim at the British soldiers. He ducked behind the door of a compartment as more bullets whizzed past him, missing him by mere inches. Where was Parineeta? Was she all right? He propelled himself from the other side of the compartment and stepped back onto the road.

The gunfire continued, but he couldn't stay put any longer. He had to get to her. What did she think she was doing? The British soldiers were rushing toward her. She turned around every few yards to shoot behind her, just enough to keep them off her trail but not enough to prevent the distance between her and the soldiers from narrowing with each passing second.

Warren raced toward a compartment in front of her incoming path. He lifted himself into one of the open compartments and peered out from behind the metal shelter. As soon as she passed by his hiding spot, he pulled her in.

She gasped for breath in his arms, her gun still smoking. "Ammunition," she wheezed. "I'm running low on bullets. I need to reload."

He groaned. There was no way he was letting her go out there again. "Who are you trying to kill, Parineeta?" he demanded, snatching the gun out of her hand.

She reached for it, but he held it up and away from her. She narrowed her eyes, unable to bring herself up to his height. "I am not going to kill anyone! I need to tell the passengers to close their windows."

"I'm sure they will. You don't need to fire a gun in the air in order to get their attention." He wasn't going to let her die out there. Still, he brought the gun back down, allowing her to grab it from his hands.

"It is my own decision if I choose to die for this fight." Her chin tilted upward, in that defiant motion that both irritated and amused him at the same time.

"And I will not let that happen." He wanted more than anything to take that gun out of her hands and keep her safe with him until the area outside the train was clear to leave. But he couldn't control her. He gazed down at the rebellious woman, her plait nearly undone from her running and her cheeks flushed from excitement. She wouldn't listen to him even if he tried. He loved that about her.

Love. The word shocked him. When had he ever admitted to loving a woman before? He frowned. *Now is not the time to consider that.* He scanned outside the compartment, pushing Parineeta behind him while he checked to make sure they could join the others.

Several soldiers passed by their compartment, and Warren reached out to fire his gun when she pushed his arm down. Her gaze implored him.

Of course. She'd told him before the robbery started that she didn't want anyone killed. Still, easier said than done. Warren let the soldiers pass by them, praying that Dev and the others had already found a different hiding spot.

He peeked out again. From the end of the train, he could see Raj and a few other men dragging out the safe. The two struggled at first, but then other men joined them and succeeded in landing the safe on the ground. They started slamming their sledgehammers against the metal, trying to break open the container. On the other side of the train, the British soldiers were marching off in the other direction, looking for more rebels there. Thankfully, no one else seemed to be standing on that side. The coast was clear.

"It's safe now." He reached for Parineeta's hand and turned back around. "They're out there. We need to..."

His blood froze.

She stood before him, shaking in her sandals. A man in a British soldier's uniform and a droopy mustache pressed the barrel of his gun against her forehead, a crazed look in his eyes. Warren swallowed hard. He recognized the soldier. This man had been one of his own troops while undercover at the fort.

The soldier cocked his head in the direction of a door leading to the next train compartment. "Got in while you were looking outside. All the men know about your treachery, *General*," the man spat. His upper lip curled in disgust as he pressed the barrel against her head, harder.

She winced. Warren's stomach plummeted.

"Put your gun down. She's innocent." He tried to keep his voice even, his gaze darting back and forth between his former soldier and his current love. "I said, put your gun down."

The soldier's whole hand shook, including his finger over the trigger. "You're all brigands! You and your savage Indian gang of dacoits!"

"Not brigands. Revolutionaries."

"Why stick your neck out for a little coolie?" The man took his pistol away from Parineeta and turned it toward Warren. The barrel was aimed directly at the middle of his forehead.

"She's not a coolie." All Warren could think about was landing his right fist across the hollow of the soldier's cheek and watching his body wipe the floor clean.

"Then what is she?" The soldier sneered. He cocked the barrel of his revolver. "You going to marry her, *General?* You going to actually give this darkie the time of day?"

Warren tried not to look at her. If this was where he was to die, he couldn't bear to see the look in her eyes when this man pulled the trigger. "She has a name. And your blood is no better than hers."

"Ha! Then you deserve to..."

BANG!

Chapter Nine

The man's eyes widened suddenly. He dropped his gun and, with a low groan, crumpled to the ground. His legs splayed out behind him, while a fresh wound oozed from the lower part of his back. Blood was everywhere, covering the walls of the compartment and splattering a red design on Warren's beige shirt.

Parineeta's eyes were wide, and her jaw had dropped, as if she was surprised at what had happened herself. The revolver she held in her hands was still shaking, from the force of a fatal bullet this time.

"*Bhagwan.*" Her hand shook. The revolver dropped from her hands and clattered to the floor. She gasped, holding her face in her hands. "What have I done? Oh, what have I done?"

He stepped around the man and pulled her into his arms. He shushed her, attempting to soothe her by running his hands over her wavy hair. She leaned her head against him, shuddering as the tears streamed down her cheeks and onto his kameez.

"I killed him, Warren, I killed him." She chanted it over and over like a mantra, until she broke out into a fresh sob.

He pressed a kiss to her forehead. "You had no other choice. He would have killed us otherwise."

Parineeta then stood still, as if considering his words.

"You saved my life," he whispered.

She looked up. The corners of her eyes were still wet with tears, but her gaze had refocused. Her tone became firm once more. "And you were willing to save mine."

"Guess we're even now." His heart constricted in his chest at the petite girl in his arms. She was stronger than he ever knew was possible. He dipped his head toward hers, edging closer to her lips.

Ashfaqulla appeared in the entrance of the doorway. He held no guns, only a crowbar he'd managed to acquire somewhere. "Raj has the money. We need to go, *now!*"

Warren stepped away from Parineeta, even as Ashfaqulla sped away from them. He rubbed the back of his neck, and she coughed. His eyes darted from the metal walls of the compartment behind her to her arms folded over her chest. Her shoulders slumped forward, but a smile remained on her features.

Raj waited outside in a clearing, along with the others. Her brother and several other men carried sacks over their shoulders, which jingled with coins as they ran away from the train. Several men had bundled the money in old rugs.

"*Inquilab zindabad!*" Raj chanted as they fled.

The others chanted after him. The daylight had faded into the darker shades of evening, but Warren still saw the triumphant expressions of each of the men.

A grin spread out across his own face. *Inquilab zindabad*—Long live the revolution.

He grabbed Parineeta's hand. She looked up sharply then toward the direction of the others. He felt her grip relax in his hand when she realized no one had seen them.

The men ran slightly ahead of them, whooping for joy as they carried away their loot. Some of the men swung the bags at their sides, while others placed them over their shoulders. A kind of fever had swept over the whole group, consuming in its power and addictive in its rush as the unison chant formed a song in his soul. He felt the revolutionary spirit thrumming through his body, coursing through his veins.

She squeezed his hand, and the two of them chanted together. "*Inquilab zindabad! Inquilab zindabad!*"

•••

They'd continued their journey for several hours before they stopped for a break. The men convinced Warren to help them distribute the sacks and rugs of money before they carried them into Lucknow.

Raj set his bag down, and his friends set about reallocating the funds into different sacks. Ashfaqulla knew of a safe house waiting for them in Lucknow; they could store the loot there and rest for the night.

Parineeta intended to help them until her brother stepped in front of her. Both of his hands were thrust into the length of his pockets, and his gaze considered her beneath arched brows.

She gulped. "Hello, Raj."

"I am starting to wonder why you helped this American." He spoke with slow deliberation, as if each word had a separate purpose.

The hairs on the back of her neck bristled. "I already told you. Once we reach Lucknow, he will tell me of how the British view our Hindustan Republican Association. He said he will tell me any information I ask of him."

"And then?"

Parineeta felt the pointed edge of her brother's question. The two words stung more than salt sprinkled over a fresh wound. She knew what he was implying, yet she remained silent. How was she supposed to answer a question she didn't even dare ask herself?

"I said, what happens after he gives you the information?"

She swallowed hard. "He can do whatever he wishes."

"You want him to stay." It was a statement, not a question. Her brother searched her gaze. She had no doubt he would find the answer he'd already suspected. "You're hoping he decides to stay with us."

"He has no reason to." She felt a lump rise in her throat. In all likelihood Warren would leave, travel back to America, and serve another mission somewhere else in the world.

"You could ask him to stay."

Her cheeks flushed. "Beg? Never." She could not implore him to stay with her, not the same way she'd heard her mother had begged of her father. Even the possibility of it made her toes curl within her sandals. She may have lost her heart, but she wasn't going to lose her dignity.

"No one said anything about begging, *didi*." Raj sighed.

"Mother begged. Look what good it did her." She hadn't wanted her tone to sound so bitter, yet the callousness was unmistakable. "I swore to myself I would never be in her position."

"Warren and your father are not the same person. Mother made mistakes, but she was never afraid of love."

"I am not afraid."

Her brother looked skyward, as if the heavens would give him the right words. "No one can be strong all the time."

So what if she felt a tiny ounce of fear? And what if she was terrified of asking Warren to stay and hearing him reject her? "We agreed to only accompany each other to Lucknow and then part ways. That was the end of our bargain."

"Dev told me you turned down his marriage proposal earlier today. He sounded disappointed."

She could hardly call his statement a proposal. No man so fixated on the purity of her blood could offer a happily married life to a woman. "Most men possess an idea of me as half-caste and undesirable. Dev cannot see past my birth."

"Why do you sound so calm?" Her brother furrowed his brow. "Admitting your half-caste status always seemed such a burden to you. You told me once that it was a source of shame, did you not? That it caused you to suddenly be aware of how different you were from everyone else."

She remembered that confession. She'd shared the insecurity with her brother years ago, after another woman in the village had told her that she didn't belong anywhere. Dev had brought up her birth as if she'd no other choice but to marry him. "I used to think no man could look past my heritage. It's never been a source of pride for me, brother. But now it is no longer a weakness."

He nodded. "You are right. Dev, maybe. But not all men see you in that way."

His next unspoken words hung in the air between them. *Not all men…not Warren.* Raj turned back to the other revolutionaries, leaving Parineeta alone with her thoughts.

Danger. The word had never scared her before. She'd welcomed all types of danger, from lying to her grandmother about where she was to listening in on her brother's meetings to spying on the (supposed) British general. But one look at Warren set off warning alarms through her mind. One look at him convinced her that danger could be terrifying after all.

She caught Warren's eye. He stopped talking to Ashfaqulla to meet her gaze, and Ashfaqulla backed away as soon as she began walking forward. The second she reached him, she threw her arms around him without a word. The security she felt in his embrace almost took her breath away each time he held her. All these years she'd spent searching for a place she belonged. That old woman from her past was wrong. Parineeta did belong somewhere. But it was with a person, not a place.

He stepped backward at the sudden force around his waist. "What's all this for? What did your brother say?"

The urge to ask him to stay tugged at the end of her tongue. She tried to will the question out of her, to finally make itself known. Here was her chance!

"Are you all right?"

She nodded against his arm. Something was lodged in her throat, preventing the query from surfacing. Wrapping her arms around Warren to prevent him from letting her go was one matter, but begging him out loud to stay with her was another. How could she keep him from his own destiny?

"Good. Ashfaqulla told me we could reach Lucknow within the hour if we hurried."

She held him tighter. "That is wonderful," she lied.

The hour to Lucknow was the fastest Parineeta had ever experienced. Every step seemed to move more quickly than the one before it, and the minutes blended together until she spotted the winding streets and bustle of the Lucknow market.

The boys finished packaging the money into the safe house while she stood on guard outside. No British soldiers had reached the city yet or at least none that they had seen. She knew if they were lucky, they would be able to escape early tomorrow morning without being noticed.

After the last of the bags were placed inside the house, she went inside to check on the boys. Dev, Ashfaqulla, Bismil, and the others seemed content. Even with the afternoon sun still hanging in the sky, a few had begun napping. Her brother and another boy sat in one corner of the warehouse, polishing their guns next to the money bags while their friends slept.

Yet there was no sign of Warren.

Parineeta tried to ignore the alarm bells ringing in her head. She started in the direction of her brother, her heart weighing heavier with each step she took. "Have you seen Warren?"

Raj shook his head. He said nothing, but his features softened. She didn't have to be a psychic to know he didn't expect Warren to return.

His friend next to him pointed to the large wooden door where she had entered. "He left about an hour ago. Didn't say why, just left. I thought he went out to say something to you."

She resisted the urge to sink to her knees. Instead, she raced back outside. She scanned the end of the street from both sides.

Maybe he'd stayed in the area. She dashed around the corner, checking the next avenue. Still no sign of him.

She sighed. Her sandals dragged against the paved road and through the dizzying maze of alleys. Perhaps if she just kept looking, perhaps he was standing on the next corner...

She shut her eyes against the last rays of the sun. He hadn't even said goodbye. She swore she would never be her mother; she would never allow herself to love a man who would leave her.

Then why did she feel so abandoned?

• • •

NBCI operative Jerry Albright spun the globe with a single flick of his thumb and forefinger. The world beneath his hand twirled around on its axis, changing direction at his command with a simple tap of his finger.

"You could go anywhere now, Warren." Jerry's voice sounded light. He continued to spin the globe in an absentminded manner. The coffee on his oak desk was forgotten at the prospect of new adventures. "God knows I'm dying to get out of here. Moscow was better. I can stand the cold, you know. Humidity? Not so much."

"This country suited me just fine." Warren set his jaw and leaned back against the hard-backed chair. "I don't think I'll be doing any more traveling."

The globe stopped spinning. "Can't change that. They'll reassign you."

"Who's 'they'?"

"The FBI. NBCI underwent some changes last year. Less focus on anarchists, more focus on investigation back home."

"There won't be any more reassigning for me, I'm afraid. I'm staying in India."

"Just because your identity was discovered doesn't mean the FBI no longer wants you." Jerry shrugged. "All that matters is that you made it out alive. Identity exposure happens to all of us at some point."

Warren took a long sip from his coffee. He'd once looked at that globe in the same way Jerry did. At the single mention of a reassignment, he'd be all packed and in some new place by the end of the month. He would explore new cities, try new measurement collection techniques, and speak different languages. The thrill of the job always caused him to accept whatever reassignment he was given. Several months, several years—each location had a time limit. When his time was up, he left with no questions asked.

But then he'd never had any reason to stay in a certain place, either.

"I'm not working with the NBCI, FBI, whatever it is anymore." His gaze drifted from the globe to his former fellow operative. "I belong here. Please tell the agency about my resignation."

Jerry laughed. "You have to be joking! Why would you stay behind?"

It began with the robbery, the feelings of independence and hope that had coursed through him. The fight for freedom had become his fight as well. "I've found a reason to stay."

The other agent clasped his hands together. He propped his elbows on his desk, the starched cuffs folded up before his wrists with neat precision. "Are you sure this is what you want?"

"I was assigned this job in India. This was always going to be my last assignment."

Jerry furrowed his brow. "You always knew this was going to be it? What, this whole thing was planned out?"

"No. I definitely didn't plan my last few weeks here." The corner of Warren's mouth quirked upward as the flashing eyes of a tanned beauty entered his thoughts. "But this is what I've decided. I'm staying."

"I will relay back to the bureau your information about how Raj Singh is not an anarchist threat." The man sitting opposite him sighed. "I hope you're making the right choice, my friend."

He'd never been so sure of a decision. Warren stood from his chair and walked away from the table. As he opened the door to leave, the other agent called something out to him. Warren glanced over his shoulder.

Jerry leaned back in his chair with his feet propped up on his desk and his hands tucked behind his head. He repeated the words to Warren again as he saluted him.

"You'll be missed, Agent Warren Khan!"

He smiled. It had been a while since someone had called him by his real name.

Chapter Ten

The moon hung high over the quiet streets of Lucknow. Crickets chirped, and a few dogs barked. But no roaring motorcycles sped down the streets, and no marching British soldiers interrupted her sleep.

Not that sleep had been easy to find.

Parineeta pulled her knees against her chest and smoothed out the skirt of her sari over her legs. She pushed back her veil as she tilted her head up to look at the sky. She'd often imagined shapes in the stars, catching memories and scenes with nothing more than the string of a few lights. But there were so few stars visible over the city that she could barely count them, much less make shapes out of them. Maybe that was how drowsiness would find her for the night.

She squeezed her eyes shut then opened them again. The effort was useless. Counting stars would not help her find peace of mind any more than attempting to stop the thoughts of Warren from entering her head.

Focus on the money. After the boys woke up, she and her brother's friends had spent all afternoon counting how much cash they'd stolen: more than 10,000 rupees. If that didn't create public attention, nothing would. The boys talked about splitting up, going into different directions to avoid capture for a few months and then meeting again later once more men in the HRA had been trained.

Her brother was returning to work in the general's house since he'd heard a new general moved in. A few of the other freedom fighters were headed to the west to meet with more members of the Hindustan Republican Association and continue plotting. He didn't believe the police would find them, but it was better for everyone to go their own separate ways until the next plan was made. Dev even offered his proposal of marriage a second time. She cringed at the thought of accepting him. To think that only a few weeks ago she would have accepted his criticism of her as fact. She had been so sure all men would never see past her race.

Not all men. *Not Warren.*

She shut her eyes again, pressing her lashes against her skin as hard as she could. If only there was a way to erase all feelings for him. She opened her eyes and groaned. A mirage that looked just like Warren walked up the street toward her.

Of course. She was even imagining him!

Her imagination conjured him up to look nearly the same as she'd last seen him: blood-stained kameez, beige sandals, and a smile lighting up his aristocratic features. The only difference was that the dust that had settled over his face had been cleaned up, as if he'd used someone's washing bin. His dark hair swept back from the wind, contrasting his olive skin.

Her imagination willed him closer and closer. *That's odd.* She blinked again, trying to push the dream away. Surely she could control her own visions.

The mirage of Warren stopped in front of her. "Parineeta, what's wrong?"

The dream even spoke!

"No, you can't be real," she muttered. She resisted the urge to poke him in the leg to test his existence. He couldn't be there. The real Warren left hours ago.

He sat down next to her. "Why wouldn't I be real?"

The deep baritone of his voice sent a rush up her spine. He sounded real. He reached for her hand and interlaced her fingers with his. She squeezed his palm, and he squeezed back.

Definitely real.

"I thought you had already left."

He frowned. "Why would I leave?"

She pulled her hand away from his. "The reason you came to Lucknow was to speak to another agent, you said."

"Yes. I met with another operative earlier today."

"Are you here to say goodbye now?" Parineeta clasped her hands together. She brought her knees closer to her chest and spread out her sari over her ankles. But she felt ridiculous, covering a piece of skin he had already seen before. "Do you leave tomorrow morning?"

"No."

"No?" She leaned forward. Had she misheard him?

Warren cleared his throat. He leaned back, extending his arms behind him and laying his palms flat against the dirt. "Listen, there's something I need to tell you. My real name is not, as you know, Warren Carton."

She pursed her lips. "Clearly. So?"

"My real name is Warren Khan."

Her eyes widened. All this time and she'd had no idea. "You must be joking. You look...you look..."

"My mother was white. My father was half-Indian." He picked up her hand again, and this time she didn't let her palm slip from his grasp. He stroked the top of her fingers with his thumb as he spoke. "I was born here in India. I grew up in my father's village."

"Why did you move away?"

She saw his Adam's apple bob up and down before he continued. "My mother's father never approved of her marriage. After my parents died, he sent me away to America. I was still a child when my parents passed away."

Parineeta considered his words for a minute. He had seemed eager to join Raj's friends for the robbery. "So you joined this mission to become a freedom fighter?"

He chuckled. "No, I did not. I was assigned my location. Over time, I noticed the effects of the independence movement."

"I had no idea you were part Indian." Sure, he was more tanned than most of the other British soldiers and his hair was darker, but his American accent had established him as a foreigner. She would have never guessed he had been born here.

"I've never let my race define my identity." Warmth spread from the tops of her knuckles, up through her wrist, and along her arms until her whole body felt alight with the glow of his touch. "But I know what it's like to grow up feeling like you don't belong anywhere."

"I always felt alone when I was growing up." The words tumbled out of Parineeta's mouth before she could stop them. "I've never known anyone else who belonged to two different worlds before. Everyone else knew what family they belonged to and what traditions to believe."

"And what do you believe?"

"I believe in the Indian independence movement." She grabbed Warren's hand with her other palm and looked up into his eyes. She believed that he did, too. "Where do you think you belong?"

"That's easy. Alongside you, in the fight for independence."

Her arm dropped to her side. She scanned his expression, checking for any signs of deception or teasing.

But his tone remained serious. "When I was running with all of you and chanting, I've never had that feeling before. That feeling of complete belonging was foreign to me."

"Until today?"

"Yes. I want to keep fighting for independence and against injustice. I've witnessed—and commanded—some of the racial injustice firsthand during my time here. It's high time I fought against it."

Parineeta leaned forward and clutched his arm. "This fight is dangerous. The independence movement could take many years to succeed."

"Does it scare you?" The gleam in Warren's eyes convinced her that he already knew her answer.

"Nothing scares me."

"That's because you're crazy. *Pagal ladki.*"

"Crazy? You're calling me crazy?" She lifted up her forearm as if to strike him. He laughed and held up his hand to block her blow. With gentle pressure, he lowered her arm.

"Maybe you are." The corner of his mouth turned upward. "But this former general wouldn't want his revolutionary any other way."

She sighed. "I have dedicated myself to the independence movement. There will be no more village life for me." She stared up at the luminescent moon above them. Somehow even the stars shined brighter all of a sudden. "We will be leaving Lucknow tomorrow. My brother believes the authorities will not find us if we split up for the time being."

"Where will you go?"

"In Cawnpore, there will be an annual session of the Indian National Congress." Parineeta rested her head against the space between his shoulder and the nape of his neck. "I want to be involved with the politics as well."

"And may I accompany you?"

She couldn't stop the smile from spreading across her features. "Perhaps."

"Whatever we do, we will do together." He kissed the top of her forehead then pointed to the sky. "See those stars?"

She nodded.

"They always keep moving across the night sky—during the night, during the week, during the month. They don't settle down because they've found no reason to stay in one place for long."

"What about them?"

Warren leaned closer and closer to her, until a slight turn of his head would land her lips on his. "That is who we used to be. But now we've found something here."

"We've found our purpose."

She pressed her lips against his. The tenderness swept her away, carrying her past the stars and into his warm embrace.

She knew they'd found more than their purpose. They'd found each other.

More from This Author
(From *One Last Letter* by Pema Donyo)

Dearest Eve,

I hope this letter finds you. I'm praying you write back to this one, Eve, because Lord knows I've been spending way too much time writing to you and not enough time helping your father out. Spelling's improved, though. I can say that much. You taught me well.

Do you remember that, Eve? When the sun was down and I'd sneak out to your front porch and you would meet me there? Back when your dad didn't have that big old guard dog, back when you taught me how to read and write by lantern behind your house?

I hope you remember that. Memories of you are all I seem to have nowadays. I can't ever forget your face, but I'm sure the years have changed it a bit. You could send a picture, you know. My address hasn't changed.

Or you could send a letter. I know you're busy with school and all that, but I'm starting to feel like you've forgotten me.

I'm still back here at Hamilton, Texas. I'm still waiting.

Say something, Eve.

—Jesse

Jesse Greenwood looked up from the paper he was writing on to the blue sky in front of him. *A year.* A whole year since he'd seen her long black hair flying behind her as she raced across the field on the back of a horse, challenging her mount with verbal commands and physical kicks every chance she found. A whole year since she'd made him promise he would keep writing to her while she was away. A year since he'd spoken to her at all.

Maybe she didn't receive his letters. The idea had dawned on him before, especially when he was all by himself out on the ranch. Maybe her father kept the letters from him. Maybe someone at that fancy school of hers burned them before they could reach her hands.

He watched the herd of cattle graze on the pasture. The cattle were lazy, chewing cud all day and staring blankly at any lone cowboy who tried to herd them. They didn't worry about not receiving letters.

One letter out of—how many was it now? Thirty? Forty? Every spare moment he had ended up filled with writing to her. Maybe it was time to give up. He swallowed feelings of surrender. No, he'd promised to write.

Jesse sighed. After putting away the paper, he headed back toward his horse. Promises sure were hard to keep when you didn't know if the other person gave a damn. As he herded the cattle to head back to the ranch, the sun began to set. The fading light filled the sky with deep purple and orange hues. There was no way Eve could see that sunset off on the East Coast, where the sun probably never shined and children probably never learned how to race horses.

"Hey, Greenwood!"

He turned his head at the call of his name. Another one of the ranch hands, Preston, rode up next to him. The beginnings of a beard peppered Preston's jawline, reminding Jesse that he hadn't shaved in days. He didn't really shave anymore, ever. There didn't seem much incentive when Evelyn wasn't around.

As if reading his mind, Preston slapped Jesse's back and whistled low. "Your girl's coming home."

Jesse nearly dropped the folded letter in his hand. He tucked it into his pocket instead and tightened his hands on his reins for a better grip. "What did you just say?"

Preston arched an eyebrow and grinned. "You heard me, all right. Evelyn Lancaster's headed back to Hamilton."

While his eyes never strayed from the cattle he and Preston were taking back to the ranch, Jesse's body was on autopilot. With the trail to the ranch memorized, his mind whirred, trying to process the information Preston had given him.

Preston headed off in the opposite direction and took the cattle from the other side as another ranch hand opened up the gates. Jesse waited until Preston finished trotting around the extent of the corral. Either Preston's daily check of the corral needed more time today, or he was just taunting Jesse. He stepped out of the stirrups and jumped to the ground, his hand drifting to his pocket where the letter lay in the process. When Preston finished, he finally let go of his reins and also dismounted.

The two guided their horses back toward the stable. Jesse could feel Preston's eyes studying his expression. "I ain't lying. She's back for good."

His throat felt dry. "How would you know that?"

Preston chuckled. "Heard it from the big bug himself. 'Make sure Blue Star is ready, Preston.' That was when I asked. Boss said she's come back to be married. Heard she's become real pretty now, too." Preston took off his beige hat as they stepped out of the stable. Once they reached the house, he stamped his feet on the mat in front of the porch door. A plume of dust flew up from the mat in a cloud, a tribute to the day's work on the ranch. He brushed off the dirt from his clothes, taking extra care to appear presentable.

Jesse raised an eyebrow.

Preston shook his head. "Not trying to make myself look good for Evelyn—she's your girl."

Jesse took off his black hat and stepped inside. "Not talking about her, Preston. I know who you're trying to impress." Preston Dean had been chasing Jesse's baby sister for the last year, not that Jesse approved. He figured Preston's interest in her would fade, the way the rest of his friend's annual infatuations did. Thankfully, Loretta Greenwood hadn't shown any interest in him, and Jesse planned to keep it that way.

"She's not too much younger than Eve was when you two got all lovey-dovey. If I wanted to do the same with your sister, then I—"

Jesse shot his friend a warning look, but Preston smirked. "You just wait and see. Loretta will come around."

The two walked down the hallway of the bunkhouse Mr. Lancaster had provided for his ranch hands. Their heavy footsteps thudded against the wooden flooring. The hallway was empty, and Jesse guessed all the other cowboys were eating at the cookhouse.

Beds lined the back of the bunkhouse, each one stacked a level on top of each other to conserve space. The boss hadn't provided them with much, but a clean bed was all Jesse needed. It had been hard trying to find a job after his parents died; landing a place as a ranch hand had also meant Loretta could work in the kitchen and sleep in the big house, which seemed more than generous to him.

He swallowed hard and pulled the letter from his pocket. The folds seemed to ruin it somehow, and he smoothed the paper with care on the nearest table. So she'd returned to be married. His heart knew who she wanted. She'd told him so; she didn't want to marry anyone else.

His heart beat faster, and he felt perspiration begin to gather in the base of his palms. Her father must have come around after all.

There was a knock at the door from the back entrance. Too early for the other ranch hands to return from supper. Preston nearly darted forward to answer the door, but Jesse shot him a stern look. If it really was Loretta at the door, he certainly didn't want Preston greeting her.

He set his black hat on the table before he walked over to the doorway. What was she thinking? It really wasn't proper for his sister to come to the bunkhouse at this time.

He opened the door. "Loretta, I told you for the last time to stop encouraging Preston into believing that . . ."

His voice trailed off once his eyes recognized the figure standing on the other side of the doorway. His eyes widened, and he felt his pulse racing.

The girl at the door was definitely not Loretta.

"Hello, Jesse."

• • •

Evelyn Lancaster wanted to run away as fast as possible.

It was a mistake. It was one colossal, gargantuan mistake. Worse than Athens ordering the death of Socrates. Worse than Persephone being kidnapped by Hades. What did she think she was going to do? Seconds ticked by as she found herself unable to say anything more. Her mouth felt dry. What was she supposed to say?

He'd changed, more than she would have ever imagined possible. The boyish frame was filled out, and extra years working on the ranch had defined the muscles in his arms under his coarse brown shirt. He'd even grown taller—past six feet, she guessed. His shoulders were broader, and his cheekbones seemed more pronounced than before. His face carried even more of an aristocratic air, but his body seemed undeniably more masculine.

Yet the expression was the same. Jesse Greenwood's same reticent, admiring expression hadn't changed as he continued to stare at her like she was hand-blown glass. His brown hair still flopped lightly in front of his eyes, causing him to brush it away.

"Hey, Eve."

She winced. She hadn't heard that nickname since she'd left Hamilton, Texas, for the female seminary in Massachusetts. No one at her women's college ever called her Eve. During classes she'd been "Miss Evelyn" and "Miss Lancaster."

She cleared her throat. She'd anticipated the awkwardness but not the simple difficulty in forming words. "I returned home a few hours ago. I thought I should stop by and say hello. Is Preston here? Are any of the other ranch hands here?"

Jesse blinked. He didn't respond for a few seconds. The adoring expression morphed to one of disbelief. "Eve, did you get my letters?"

She bit her lip. "I did." Evelyn resisted the urge to embrace him. Doing so would only make it harder to answer his questions with a lie. Instead, she stood rooted to the spot. She wouldn't move a muscle; there was too much she could regret. "They were nice letters. Thank you. But I burned them."

His eyes became cool steel, all traces of admiration in his eyes melting away. "Burned them? But you . . ." His jaw was set. "Eve, why didn't you write me back?"

"I was busy." She tore her eyes away from Jesse's searing gaze and tried to look behind his shoulder. The sinking feeling in her chest was surely no more than an echo of the past. She needed to leave before all rationality left her. "Just let all the other ranch hands know I stopped by."

"Stop. Eve, I said stop." Strong hands grabbed both of her shoulders, and she looked up in alarm toward his furrowed brow and confused expression. His voice was so much deeper than she'd remembered. "That's all? You couldn't once respond to me?"

She struggled to push against him, but he held her in place. His tone was rough. It increased in volume, rising with each word that tumbled out of his mouth.

"What about the promise I made to you? When you told me that you wanted to marry—"

"Enough!" Evelyn yanked herself out of his hold and glared. She breathed deeply, as if the extra air would give her the courage she couldn't truly conjure up. "I remember what you are referring to. I did receive your letters. I thank you for them. But I did not

respond to you because whatever we had before I left for school
. . ." She gulped. The polite tone of indifference faded. "This has
to end."

The reaction was immediate. His features crumpled as she
stepped back. His jaw went slack, and she saw his hands at his side
ball into fists. He looked like someone had just punched him in
the gut. Evelyn's heart broke as she watched him step toward her.

"Neither of us has any money."

"So? We never worried before. We said we'd run away . . ."

She let out a bitter laugh. "To where? Where would we go?"

"Anywhere. Away from here." He edged closer. "You don't have
to listen to your father."

"This has nothing to do with him. This is my choice, not his."

A pause. "I wish you chose a different one."

She wished he wouldn't say anything further. The longer she
listened to him, the more her walls of resolve crumbled. Saving
the family ranch came before her personal choices.

"You are referring to a conversation from a year ago." She
smoothed out her dress, as if wiping away the wrinkles would
wipe away the intensity of the conversation. "I may have said
certain promises with foolish hope . . ."

"That wasn't foolish hope, Eve." His voice was guttural. She
swallowed when she looked away from her skirt to his clenched
fists. The muscles in his forearm tightened as he spoke. "We were
in love. We are—"

"Stop. Do not speak of that." She narrowed her eyes at Jesse.
How could he be so inconsiderate? "Four years has changed us. It
has changed my perspective."

Bitterness marked his tone. "It's given you amnesia, apparently."

If only. Evelyn pressed her lips together. Images of kissing him
by the light of the moon in the stable, sketches he made of her
behind the house, poems she read to him after they had finished

racing horses around the ranch when his hours finished. All the memories threatened to overwhelm her, and she swayed slightly.

"Know what I think?"

She bristled, and he didn't wait for her response.

"I think you're scared."

Anger flashed through her. Scared? Never. Practical? Definitely. "I am a realist, not a coward. I am giving up on you, Jesse."

He remained silent. She wanted him to reply, to say something, anything. Any words seemed better than the heavy silence that fell between them instead.

She finally looked up. His eyes met hers with a fierce glare. There was no sadness in his expression, only bitter betrayal. His fists had not unclenched. Evelyn believed that if she reached out, her palms would meet the invisible wall suddenly erected between them.

"We are not possible together, understand?" She struggled to keep her voice even. "I need to marry someone who is more financially secure, Jesse." She stepped back again, away from the barrier between them. "I understand that I told you differently before, but time has passed. It is better for both of us if we just forget . . ." Her voice lowered. "Forget we ever knew each other at all."

He didn't even slam the door. Jesse shut it with as little sound as possible, the lock barely making a noise as she heard the bolt slide into place.

She bit her lip. *If you didn't tell him now, you would have to tell him later. You did the right thing.* Those unbidden feelings, and her body's instincts, had been so much easier to suppress when she was away from him. Every muscle inside Evelyn wanted to run forward and slam her hands against the wood until he opened up and she jumped back into his arms.

Instead, she turned around and walked back toward her home.

• • •

The next few weeks blurred together in a torrent of tears and indecision. All the eligible young men in the surrounding area had asked her father for a chance to court her. Her father brought up each one at supper, highlighting their fine qualities and numerous bags of cash to their name. He never mentioned it out loud, but his message was clear: The ranch was no longer his priority, but hers as well.

But each suitor seemed so weak. None of them would last a day managing a ranch. Everyone pointed to her father's wealth as a reason for marrying her, and none seemed to show genuine interest in her beyond her physical appearance.

"If you're shaking your head because of all the potential beaus you've rejected, I am not surprised. You're wasting your time trying to choose one from that bunch." Annie Inglewood, her best friend, cast a dismissive gaze in Evelyn's direction. The redhead sat on a wooden bench next to Evelyn's vanity, admiring her own reflection in the mirror. "Have you ever considered that maybe you'll never accept any of the suitors?"

"Bosh! There are at least ten more I have not met yet." Still, she wasn't particularly enthused at the idea of meeting another ten bachelors who were most likely going to be as unappealing as the last six. "I could accept one of them."

"None of them is Jesse."

Evelyn drew in a quick intake of breath. "I need someone with more financial stability."

"Then what's wrong with the ones you've rejected?"

What was wrong, indeed? A sinking feeling settled in her stomach. "Or I could pursue a career of my own."

"I doubt Jesse would ever stop you from doing something you wanted."

Jesse this, Jesse that. When would she stop hearing his name everywhere she went in Hamilton?

Annie rolled her eyes and spun around, fixing Evelyn a critical eye. "Why are you so insistent on being married now, anyway?"

"The ranch can use all the financial support it can get." She shifted her weight on the bed, realizing the contradiction between her words and behavior. Then why couldn't she just tie herself to one of the rich fellows who expressed interest?

"Have a word with your father. I'm sure he'd listen if you just asked him for more time."

Maybe Annie did have a point. Jesse could be out of the question, but maybe her father would postpone her marriage and her list of suitors for a few years. There was no time like the present to find out. Evelyn opened the door and walked down the hallway, toward the study. Annie called out her name, but Evelyn ignored her.

She stepped inside her father's room. On one side of the study, the wall was lined with several rows of bookshelves containing dusty tomes ranging in topics from finance to law to agriculture. The sturdy spinning globe she loved so much as a child still rested on a small table in the center of the room. And behind the large oak desk, where papers determining the future of her family's ranch were strewn, sat her father.

Thomas Lancaster set down the papers in his hand when he saw her enter the room. Rarely worn glasses perched on the bridge of his nose. His forehead was creased with worry, yet he smiled when he saw his eldest. "Evelyn, what is it?"

"Father, the list of suitors . . ." She mustered up enough courage to step forward. Her father's large oak desk seemed imposing, but infinitely more intimidating was her father's expectant expression. "I think we need to talk about who I want to marry."

"Well, of course, go ahead." He gestured his hand outward.

She paused. "I have been giving some consideration to my marriage and I—"

Before she could finish, Mr. Lancaster held his palm up to Evelyn to quiet her for a moment. His gaze shifted to a point behind her. "Come right in, Greenwood."

She stood perfectly still as heavy footsteps approached her father's desk. She had to remind herself to breathe as she sneaked a look out of the corner of her eye at the tall man standing next to her.

Jesse Greenwood's expression was firm, the hard lines of his face even more stern than she'd ever seen them. He smelled of fresh morning air, dust from the trails, and a familiar musky scent that was uniquely his. Her body longed to turn her head toward him and bury her face in his shirt and wrap her arms around him—

No, that was in the past now.

He nodded to her father. "Just wanted to say goodbye, sir, before I hit the road."

Her father smiled at Jesse. Or rather, she knew, he smiled at the lack of interaction he saw between Jesse and Evelyn. "I wish you the best of luck in California, boy. Whenever you want to return to Texas, my ranch is always willing to hire a hand with your skills."

Her eyes widened, but she didn't dare look at Jesse. Surely there was some mistake. He couldn't really leave. Her stomach plummeted.

He just couldn't.

"Loretta's staying, though. She's happy here. I'll send money to her soon as I get settled out West." He placed his hat on his head and adjusted the rucksack over his shoulder. "Much thanks for the horse you provided me, sir."

"It's the least I can do for your years of service, Greenwood. Best of luck on your journey."

She scowled. More like the least he could do to show his appreciation that Jesse was leaving his ranch.

Jesse nodded again, and then turned to leave. He didn't even glance in her direction. It was as if she was invisible to him now.

She heard his footsteps leave the room, felt the air shift as his familiar scent faded, and wanted nothing more than to run after him as fast as she could.

Instead, she stayed still.

Praise for *One Last Letter*:

"...friendship, broken love, regrets, family, sacrifice, renewed love, and choices ... I recommend this novel to anyone who is looking for a lighthearted, feel-good romance."—5 stars, *History from a Woman's Perspective*

"There's romance, and then there's heart-pounding, breathless, fabulous, fantastic *romance*. Pema Donyo's *One Last Letter* falls in that category ... I can't wait to read it over again."—4 stars, *The Canon*

"...young love becoming true love ... a lighthearted love story with passion. I am looking forward to the next book Pema writes."—5 stars, *Let's Get Romantical*

In the mood for more Crimson Romance?
Check out *Expressly Yours, Samantha* by Becky Lower at
CrimsonRomance.com.

Printed in the United States
By Bookmasters